MORE THAN WRITE

JAMI ROGERS

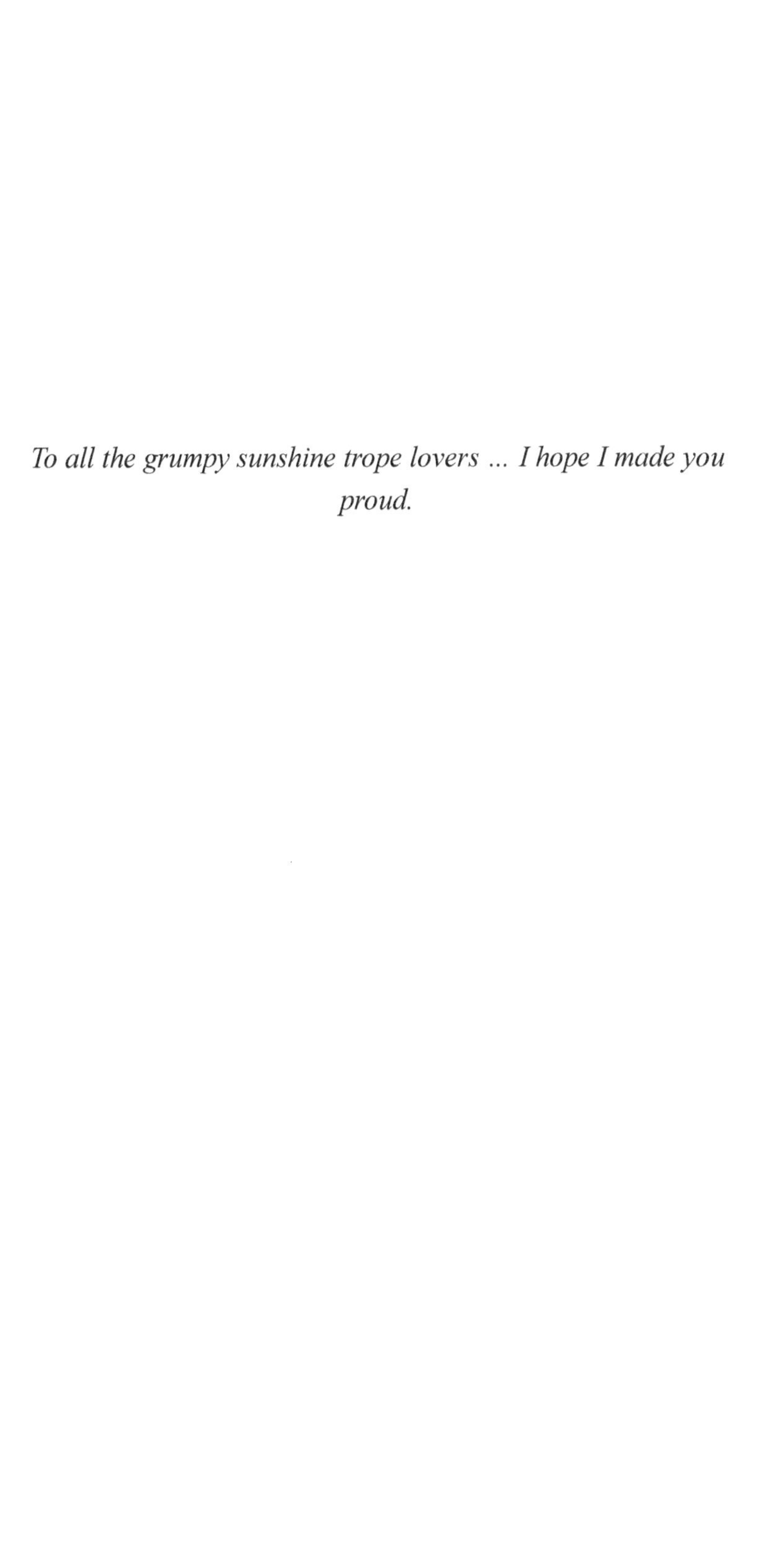

To all the grumpy sunshine trope lovers ... I hope I made you proud.

🌼 Formatted with Vellum

MORE THAN WRITE

JAMI ROGERS

CHAPTER ONE
GREER

My ass hurts.

I pick up the fifty-pound kettlebell and proceed to squat for what feels like the hundredth time.

You like working out.

You're improving your mood.

You love food.

You have a pint of Cherry Garcia ice cream in the freezer.

Moving your body is good for you.

I repeat my mantra at least three more times as I finish my set. My current client is already lying on the floor, groaning.

"Hell, Greer," he says. "Day after day, you kill me while I'm here, and for some reason, I just keep coming back."

"Well, David, that's my job."

David owns the building where I work. It started as a health and nutrition studio that my best friend Willa opened, but as the spaces on either side of her studio slowly opened, she added them to her lease. When I told her I wanted to branch into personal training in addition to nutrition, she signed me on as partner, and after many trainings and certifications, here I am.

"Of all the people you could have chosen to work out with today, I can't believe you picked me," He laughs and rolls up to sit.

I take the spot next to him, sticking my legs out straight and reach for my toes.

I take part in at least one client's workout a day. I switch it up from time to time, since no two clients have the same workout.

"I needed a challenge today."

Did I really?

Yes and no.

I needed something to push me. To trick my brain into thinking of anything other than my personal life.

That's why I love what I do so much. I control the outcome when it comes to what goes in my mouth and my body movements. If I stick to the plan, it will work. The way I take care of my body is all up to me. Only me. Do I have days at home where I eat milk and cookies and vegetable fried rice takeout? Of course I do. I don't believe in cutting out food. I believe in balance. Even if it can be a real bitch sometimes to maintain.

Plus, David's workout was an hour compared to a lot of my thirty- or forty-five-minute clients, and today, I needed the full sixty minutes of distraction.

Unfortunately for me, it didn't matter if I had a fifty-pound weight on my thighs during my wall sits. The question on my mind still remains.

Why do men have to suck so damn bad?

It shouldn't be that hard to find a good guy.

I know they're out there. My best friends are living proof that they are. I've seen them in action. I've just yet had the chance to date one.

Honestly, there was one who came close. I even went as far as to take him to a work retreat once upon a time. But he claimed I was too intense for him. He wanted a laid-back life. Not one filled with goals and working out every day and precooked meals.

I get it. My lifestyle isn't for everyone. That's just fine. No two people are supposed to live the same life or have the exact same goals. We're meant to be different, but it does help if your partner gets you, supports you, and wants you to reach your goals even if they don't look like their own. That was my only boyfriend who gave me an actual reason—shit. This is exactly why I needed the full hour of self-torture. Once I get going on this mindset, I obsess over it.

I'm not boy crazy or man crazy or whatever you want to call it. I just want to find my person and make a life with him.

It sounds a lot simpler than it really is.

"Greer." David has moved on to the next stretch. He's even grabbed water from the cooler and is offering me one. "Is everything okay?"

"Yes," I answer and stand. "That one was a doozy."

I take the water and then grab my tablet to pull up my planner.

"Your wife comes in next. Did you want me to schedule the next few sessions as a joint one?"

Typically, I train only one client at a time, but the occasional couple doesn't bother me. Especially David and Melanie. They're a fun pair. They love a good challenge against one another.

"Yeah, but don't tell her. Let's keep it a surprise."

I smile and add those notes to my schedule. He packs up his things and leaves.

I sneak into the back of the studio to make a snack just as my phone goes off. It's a text reminder that my lawn guy is coming out tomorrow at eleven.

Shoot. I have a consultation for a new client at the same time, and I don't want to reschedule.

I also can't let the yard at my brand-new house die already either.

Despite my earlier pity party, I smile and do a little dance. Owning my own home was a big goal of mine, and I did it. All on my own.

I take a bite of my chocolate and cinnamon overnight oats. Who could possibly meet the lawn guy for me?

Willa is out of town. Calla, my other best friend, is just as busy with her own business, and Paige is visiting her brother. I bet Nora could do it.

I pull up her contact info and press the call button.

"Hey," she answers on the first ring. "I was just about to call you and change my appointment tomorrow morning."

"Is everything okay?" I grab my planner again.

"Yes, I just had a client call me with last-minute changes so tomorrow is going to be slammed."

Nora owns her own marketing company and specializes in working with authors. I know how important clients can be, so Nora is clearly out.

"Okay, no problem. I'll text you a few options for other openings I have this week, but it's pretty slim."

"You're the best. Now, what did you call for?"

"Oh, I have the lawn guy coming tomorrow, but I have a new client. I was going to see if you could meet him."

"Oh, I'm sorry, babe. Ask Simon. He's right there."

Ah, yes, my neighbor. He'll act like this small favor of letting someone into my backyard is a big inconvenience.

He's grumpy like that.

But Simon Stone is Calla's brother, and that's the only reason I'd even consider asking him.

"Yeah, I probably will. I just know he's busy."

"So are you. Honestly, he just has to open the gate for them. Ask him."

I could probably just leave the gate unlocked, but ick. It would drive me crazy all day knowing anyone could get into my space. I can't do it.

"I will."

"Okay, great. Let's get dinner and drinks as soon as everyone is back in town."

"Sounds great. Bye, Nora."

As soon as we hang up, I finish eating my midmorning snack and then glance at the clock. I have a lunch date, and if I leave now, that'll give me an hour to get ready with time to spare for visiting my neighbor. I'd call him, but we've only talked on the phone once, and that was months ago for his son, Grey. We'd met for dinner to go over some nutrition plans because Grey is getting into football and asked his dad if he could talk to a professional about the diet he should be on to set himself up for success. Honestly, it was the cutest thing. The fact we had this meeting at a restaurant that served unlimited chips and salsa was even better.

I push my bike, which I ride to and from work—downtown Wind Valley is only a ten-minute bike ride from my house—out the front door of the studio and lock up.

I remember that dinner like it was yesterday. Simon barely spoke. It was hard to get a word in with Grey talking and telling me all his goals for middle school and high school. He's only ten but talks like he's older. I loved that he has a plan and goals. Simon is very self-driven, so it makes sense that his kid is the same way. In the end, I gave him a few weeks of meal plan ideas, and we went our separate ways.

I'll have to ask Simon if those plans worked out for Grey.

I ride down Main Street, waving at a few random people before I turn onto the street that takes me back into the neighborhood where I live.

I wasn't born or raised in Wind Valley, but I went to college here and never left. Those people, the ones I don't even know who just waved at me, are the reason why. People here are just kind and friendly. It makes for a peaceful place to live.

The men though? Slim pickings.

However, I have high hopes for my lunch date. He's new to this area. I met him through an app, and he loves that I only schedule clients in the morning and the occasional evening, leaving my days open. Honestly, I didn't plan that from the beginning. I just have a lot of nine-to-five clients who can only train outside that, so thus, my schedule was created.

Still, his support on my out-of-the-ordinary schedule was nice. Obviously, that's not all I picked him on, but it was a perk.

I near my house, and my eyes trail in on my neighbor's front porch the way they always do.

Simon is sitting at his little white two-person table with

his laptop open in front of him and a glass of water next to it. Every day when I come home, he's in this spot. Laptop and water and all. I mean, it has to be water because it's a clear glass with clear liquid, and with his physique, I doubt he drinks much else besides a beer here or there at a friend's barbeque. Even though I wouldn't go as far to say Simon and I are friends, we do share a lot of them.

His gaze lifts from his laptop, and his eyes zero in on me.

"Hey, Simon." I smile and wave as I ride past his house. "It's so nice out today."

I hold my smile with confidence but cringe on the inside. I've said the same thing to him every day since I moved in a month ago. And each day when I ride by with my signature greeting, he just watches me without saying a word.

What a dick comes to mind, but I don't think that's the case. I don't know what his deal is, but I've seen him with Grey, and for as grumpy as Simon might be, I know deep down, he's hiding a pretty great person.

Gross. Listen to me. Is this because I just want to see the good in a single guy?

It has to be.

I park my bike in front of my garage door and walk up the sidewalk to my front door. I pause when Simon stands, his arms raising above his head as he stretches.

Now, our houses aren't kissing, but they are close enough for me to get a good view.

He's got his back to me, but his simple light gray shirt hugs his body in all the best ways. I can see the ripples of his upper back muscles, and I hate that I like it. I could get technical, but honestly saying *look at those trapezius and deltoids* doesn't sound as sexy.

Ugh, and the way his shirt hugs his biceps is great too. He flexes and the veins in his arms make an appearance. That's hot. He reaches just a little higher, and his shirt rises, revealing two dimples in his lower back. He's wearing sweats that are so perfectly low, if he turned around, I bet I'd see that V all the girls talk about.

Moody as he may be, Simon is easily the best-looking guy I've laid eyes on.

His arms drop and he sighs, one hand running through his thick black hair. He spins, sees me watching him, and pins his dark eyes on me.

What I would give to see a smile under that perfectly groomed scruff on his face.

He clears his throat.

I let out a bubble laugh and then disappear into my house.

So what if he caught me staring at him? I should probably feel guilty, but outside of his gorgeous appearance, he's not my type. Not to mention, he's never once shown any kind of interest in me. I'm clearly not his type either.

I smile.

I like to laugh.

I like conversation.

I jog up the stairs to my room and strip out of my leggings and sports bra and then get in the shower.

Enough hot neighbor talk. I have a date waiting for me, and I have a good feeling about this one.

CHAPTER TWO
SIMON

"Dad!"

I pull my gaze from the house next door, grab my computer and water, and head inside.

"Yeah?" I holler back to my ten-year-old son, Grey, who clearly can't be bothered to just walk outside to get me.

"We need to leave soon," he says, poking his head out of the kitchen, which is straight back from the front door at the back of the house. The living room is to the left, and the stairs that lead upstairs are to my right. Most of the houses in our neighborhood have the same layout. It's how I know that Greer, one of my sister's best friends who lives next door, has a house that mirrors mine. I also know this because it was on the market for so long that I toured it once to get ideas for the books I write.

I jog up the stairs to strip off my clothes to get ready. I'd been so into a zone this morning that as soon as I woke up and worked out, I'd gone right to the front porch to get some work done.

Steamy romantic suspense is my specialty, and something about having a house that wouldn't sell right next door to me sparked ideas for an entire six-book series. I went crazy with ideas and pitched them to my agent, who got me a signed deal within a few weeks. It helps that I've had bestsellers before and that I have a good relationship with all the publishing houses I've signed with. I've never missed a deadline, and as long as I'm in control, I won't ever.

It does, however, stress me out that I was so into a zone with the whole mystery house series that I agreed to closer deadlines when I signed the contract. Two months later, with four books of the series still left to write, the house was sold and that spark for the mysteriousness has dulled. Despite having a writing high this morning, that dull mood is not a good vibe for me right now.

Part of me thinks that if I could just get inside Greer's house and walk around alone, maybe that inspiration would come back. Like, maybe somehow, I could spin the type of person who moved into the house into the story. It would be nothing like Greer because her personality doesn't scream suspenseful. Her personality is more romcom. That's not my area.

With my fingers at the waist of my sweats, I start to tug them down, then movement out of my bedroom window catches my eyes.

Greer.

In a towel.

Until Greer moved in, I had no idea how much I'd see the woman whose bedroom window is right across from mine.

Right now, our houses aren't nearly far enough apart.

Her white towel is tied in a knot in front and her hair is up in a messy bun on top of her head as she opens drawer after drawer on her dresser, clearly undecided on what to wear.

Something more than skintight leggings and a crop top or sports bra, I hope.

I swear my mind and body can just sense when she's near, and as soon as that feeling hits me, I have no control over the way my eyes find her no matter what I'm doing.

It's why I'll never comment on the way I catch her checking me out. Like earlier. I'm not sure she's aware that she does this often when she's around me. But then again, I watch her like some weirdo every day when she rides her bike home, so I guess we've sort of called a silent truce of how we will never mention it to the other.

I let out a laugh as I step into the cold water.

Fucking hell.

Grey.

That kid takes half hour-long hot showers anytime I'm outside writing. I know he does.

Love the kid to death, but that's just unacceptable.

I wash quickly, wrap a towel around my waist, and head to my room to pick out clothes. Again, my eyes drift to the window.

There was only one other woman in my life who has ever stolen my attention the way Greer does.

Grey's mom. Blair.

We met before my twenty-first birthday, fell in love quickly, and she got pregnant all within about six months. I proposed a year or so after Grey was born, and then a week before Grey's second birthday, she left for the movies with friends. Next thing I knew, an officer was at our door to tell me about the car accident.

I hate that Grey has had to grow up without his mom. I hate that she never got to see him ride his first bike or hug him the first time he broke his arm. I hate that she never got her big day with the dress that's still packed away because what if Grey meets someone and she… fuck.

I take a breath and sit on the bed.

This right here, this feeling of knowing I had something amazing and lost it is why I've never seriously dated since Blair. Have I come to terms and accepted life without her? Yes. Am I thankful for every moment we had together? Yes. But loving someone and losing them is a feeling I never want to experience again.

"Dad!" Grey walks into my room.

"Hey, buddy. Knock first, remember?"

He groans and closes the door.

"Are you almost ready?" he yells from the other side instead of knocking.

I shake my head and grab some shorts and a shirt.

"Yep."

Then I slip on some sandals, brush my teeth, comb my hair, and open my door to find him waiting.

He looks at his watch.

"You're cutting it close," he says and leads me down the straight to the kitchen.

"We're going to make it just fine."

"Football starts at noon, and soccer is at three. I need to eat a proper amount of protein before then, Dad."

"Got it."

Hence why he's rushing me out the door. I promised him a power salad from one of the local juice shops downtown before practice today.

"No more pizza. We've had it three times this week."

"Okay, *Dad*," I tease and roll my eyes behind him. "Go get your things."

"They're already in the truck."

"Go brush your teeth then."

"Done." He smiles.

I glance around the clean kitchen, then I poke my head into the living room. There are actually vacuum lines in the carpet.

Damn. Okay. He can keep his half hour-long hot showers.

He grabs a water bottle from the cabinet and starts to fill it up at the fridge.

This single dad thing is tough shit sometimes, but I got lucky. Grey is a great kid.

"Stop staring at me," he whines, and then grabs his backpack before walking out the door to the garage.

I can't help but laugh.

Seriously, who is the parent here?

I hop into the truck, and as soon as we're both buckled in, I head downtown. It's a quick drive. The juice shop is four doors down from The Space, a community workspace location that Tobias and I just recently opened up.

We grab our salads and some juices before walking to The Space. There are a few spots open near the front window, so we take them.

I can't help but be impressed with this place.

It's been busy since we opened, and honestly, if I'm not writing on my porch, this is where I like to be.

"Hey," Tobias says when he walks in. His computer bag is slung over his shoulder. "Are you working today?"

Tobias and I met in college. In fact, that's how I met all

my friends. Tobias, Beck, Hero, Zane, Beck, and I all write romance, so it was easy for us to bond in college, since it isn't something a lot of guys choose as a career.

I shake my head to answer his question. "Just eating and relaxing before camp. I'll be back while he's there, though. My next book is due in two weeks, and the one after that is due in six."

Tobias whistles. "I can't believe you did that to yourself."

I was convinced the house next door wouldn't sell. A little too convinced. Clearly.

"Can you still meet the contractor this afternoon at three?" he asks.

"Yes."

"I have soccer, Dad." Grey cuts in.

"Oh, right." I look at Tobias. "Let's move it to four."

"You have to pick me up at four," Grey adds.

Shit.

"I can move something around," Tobias says. "I'll meet him today."

"Thanks."

Tobias and I have plans to open more locations around Wyoming. So things are crazy in all areas of my life. I'm not in denial. I know I spread myself thin.

"Dad, look, it's Greer," Grey says and points out the front window with his fork. Her bike rolls to a stop in front of the window, and she waves at us. Then she climbs off her bike, leans it against the building, and pushes the door open.

My eyes take in her white shoes, her lean tan legs, and then focus on the coral dress she's wearing that cinches at the waist and features a scoop neck. She has a small gold necklace with matching earrings, and her brown hair is down now, straight. Probably to accommodate the white bike helmet she's wearing. Her bright chocolate eyes catch mine for a moment before she looks between me and my son.

I swallow and then take another bite before I say something stupid, like how fucking sexy she looks right now.

"Hey, you two. You are the exact duo I was looking for."

"Is it to give us more meal plans?" Grey asks.

"No, but I can definitely do that this weekend."

"Cool." Grey smiles, and then goes back to his Game Boy and lunch.

"I was actually looking for you," she says.

I clear my throat and look up. "What do you need?"

"I need a favor tomorrow. The lawn in my backyard is dying fast and someone is coming to look at it. I was hoping you could let them in through the side gate. Or through the house since the gate lock can be a hassle sometimes."

I'll be honest, I was only half listening until she said *go through her house*. That's the kind of help I need right now.

"Yeah, I can do that."

"Really?" She beams. "It's not a problem?"

I shake my head and look at my salad. "Nope."

"Oh, great—here's my spare key."

Gold!

"I need to get going but thank you so much."

"You look really pretty. Where are you going?" Grey asks.

"Oh, thank you. I have a lunch date."

"She looks super pretty, huh, Dad?"

I turn my head slightly to glare at my kid but pull it together quickly.

"You do. Have fun."

Greer laughs and then winks at me. "Thanks, neighbor."

I watch as she walks over to the café catty-corner from us.

"Let's go, bud."

We finish our lunch, put it in the trash, and are headed to football camp when Grey speaks up.

"Oh no, I only packed my soccer shoes!"

"What?"

"We have to go home to get my cleats."

"We don't have time to grab them."

"Call Aunt Calla."

"Calla is busy, bud. Can't you just wear your soccer shoes?"

"No, I can't."

"Why not? They're both on the field, right?"

"It's not the same. I have to have different ones. Didn't you ever play sports in school, Dad?"

It takes all I have not to roll my eyes. I sure did. His persistence in having all the right equipment is me to a tee when I was his age.

"All right, well, you'll have to be late then."

"Hurry, Dad."

I head home, driving only five miles over, and Grey runs inside to grab his shoes. While I wait in the truck, a flash of coral and white goes by my rearview mirror.

I thought she had a lunch date.

I watch as Greer parks her bike, takes off her helmet, and walks up the sidewalk to her front door. She looks over for a split second. It's not much, but it's enough for me to see the tear sliding down her cheek. She swipes it away and goes inside.

My heart instantly clutches as I reach for the door handle.

I pause and take a breath.

Not my problem.

Not my problem.

Not my problem.

Grey comes running back and barely has the door open as he says, "Drive."

I laugh. I didn't know I was his getaway driver. But I wait for him to buckle up.

"You know what I was thinking," he says as I back out of the driveway.

"What's that?" I glance at Greer's house in the rearview mirror.

I bet her date was a jackass. Clearly he was if he made her cry. That right there is just another reason I won't ever date again. I've read some pretty bad first date stories. Hell, I've written them.

"You should get an assistant," Grey says matter-of-factly as he switches out his shoes.

"For what?"

"Lots of things. Your book stuff, me, the house, the food we eat. I like clean clothes too."

"I don't need an assistant, and I always wash your clothes."

"I still think you need one. Maybe your brain needs a break."

I'm about to reply when my agent calls, the ring pausing the radio and filling the speakers.

"Doug, hey," I answer through Bluetooth.

"Simon. How's it going?"

"Good. Just headed to Grey's first day of football camp."

"Fun. Fun. I'll make this quick. Did you happen to send

those first three chapters over last night? My emails have been acting up, so I wanted to check."

I groan.

"Nope. I forgot. I'll do it as soon as I drop Grey off and open my computer."

"Sounds good. Have fun, Grey."

"Thanks, Doug!"

The call ends, and I drum my thumb against the steering wheel.

How did I forget to send those chapters?

"See?" Grey smiles at me in the rearview mirror. "An assistant could have helped you remember that."

I nod but don't say anything.

He might be onto something.

CHAPTER THREE
GREER

I hate crying.

I don't feel pretty when I do it. And I'm not talking about physical appearance. I'm talking about how it makes me feel on the inside. Weak. Broken. Like I have no control over anything in my life.

I should be able to control whether I cry or not. I should be able to control how someone makes me feel. I should be able to hold my head high and walk out a door without holding my breath, thinking that it will prevent the tears from falling.

And then the blurry ride home on my bike in the middle of the day. I couldn't keep it together.

This one thing caused a domino effect, and here I am. One day later, standing in my kitchen, staring at the little sign thing sticking out of my lawn that the yard company left.

Oh, and crying. Again.

And to think, it all started when my lunch date walked into that café. I saw him at the door, waved from my seat, and that asshole cringed and then turned and walked right back out the door.

What the hell?

One look at me and he just left. Is that real life?

Yes, yes it is, because it's mine.

The timer on my oven dings, and I swipe what I hope is my last tear of the day away and grab my potholders. Then I pull a tray of cookies out and set them on the cooking rack.

I couldn't think of any other way to thank Simon for meeting the yard guy today. Food always seems to go over well.

I glance at my open trash and glare at the burned cookies inside.

This is how my day has been. I've let yesterday's date, or lack thereof, control my emotions. I worked out with two different clients this morning to keep my mind busy and then I came home, saw that stupid sign in the grass, and cried again.

I should have rescheduled with them. To a time when I could actually make it. After all, I'm going to end up alone forever. I need to start planning my life, including stupid yard maintenance into my schedule.

I sigh.

So I decided to make Simon cookies as a thank-you and burned the first batch after getting distracted by deleting all the dating apps on my phone.

I need to just face it. The men on these apps aren't right for me. If I keep using them,

I'll be alone forever.

Ugh, I really need a new approach to my dating life. The right guy is out there. He has to be.

I give the cookies a few minutes to cool, and then I put

them on a plate, cover them with plastic wrap, and place my little thank-you note on the top.

I don't remember how old I was the first time I watched my mom do this for one of our neighbors. It's a simple note of thanks, but Mom told me that it's easy to just say the words, but something about looking at a note makes people feel different. You took a little extra time to recall how that person helped you. Plus, she'd leave them when she had to go to work early. It was her way of showing me she was thinking of me even when she wasn't there.

It seems silly, but if I give anyone anything, I always include a note.

I pick up the plate and sigh again.

I miss my mom. She was the only family I had until she passed away a couple years ago. Now it's just me.

I walk outside and cross the yard to Simon's house, cutting across his driveway to the front door.

I knock twice then set the plate on his writing table. I'm turning to leave when the door opens.

"Greer."

I spin and stumble back off the next step.

He's standing in front of me shirtless, sweat running down his abs. He dabs his forehead with a towel and then readjusts the baseball cap he's wearing.

Why is a backward cap so much hotter than when they wear them normally?

"I … um," is all I get out before I point to the cookies. "Thank you for this morning. I appreciate your help."

He glances at the plate and then his eyes slowly take me in. They start at my bare feet, trailing up my legs to my shorts and sports bra and then to my lips and eyes.

I swear his gaze flickers back to my lips before he clears his throat.

"Thanks."

"You're welcome."

He grabs the plate and is stepping back inside when the door pushes open farther.

"Greer!" Grey cheers and comes out on the porch. "Are you having a better day today?"

I glance at Simon quickly and then back to Grey.

"What do you mean?"

"I had to come home yesterday to get my cleats, and I saw you crying from the front window. Did you have a bad date?"

"Grey," Simons scolds him then looks at me. "You don't have to answer that. It's not our business."

"Sorry," Grey says, his cheeks turning rosy as he looks at the ground.

"Oh, it's fine," I say quickly. "And yes, it did. It actually didn't go at all."

"Why?" Grey asks.

"Grey!" Simons scolds again.

"It's really fine," I say. "I'm not sure. I didn't get the chance to ask him."

"What a tool." Grey shakes his head.

"Jesus," Simon whispers from behind his son. "Let's let Greer get back to her day."

"All right, do you want to come have a cookie with us?" Grey asks instead of listening to his dad.

"Oh, I made those for you."

"But we can share."

"Grey, she said no. I'm sure she's had a busy day and is ready to get back to it."

Grey nods, and normally, I'd just wave and leave myself, but honestly, being alone doesn't feel so appealing right now.

"Actually, I don't have plans. I could maybe have one cookie."

I'm aware that Simon has tried to shoo me away multiple times by now, and somewhere in here, it seems I'm inviting myself to hang out with his kid. I don't really care though. Grey is cool and I… need something to do.

"Perfect! Do you know football? Maybe you could pass the ball with me while Dad finishes up his day."

"I'd love to."

Grey runs inside, shouting for me to follow him and that he just needs to go to his room to get the ball.

"You really don't have to play with him. I'm almost done with my workout, and then I have a couple of emails to reply to, and I'll be free."

"It's fine. I need a distraction anyway." I say and step into their house.

I notice the laundry basket of clothes in the living room first. As I get farther inside, I see the vacuum in the hallway, the dishes in the sink, and the pizza boxes by the trash. It's not a mess by any means—it just feels like there are a lot of unfinished tasks.

"I, uh," Simon moves to the living room to grab the basket. "We don't have guests over much unless it's Calla or Beck or the guys."

"It's fine."

"Fine," he says slowly. "Everything is fine to you."

I shrug. "I don't know what else to say."

He studies me for a moment.

"What do you need a distraction from?"

"Got the ball!" Grey comes sprinting down the stairs, jumping over the last two. "Let's go."

Hands up, I say to Simon, "Duty calls." I follow Grey out the back door before his dad can ask me any more questions.

What do I need a distraction from?

Easy. From thinking about how I'm in my early thirties and every day that passes, I grow closer to ending up alone. To never finding love like my mom had for my dad. For never getting to pass silly memories down to my kids. To not having a family at Christmas or Thanksgiving or… the list goes on.

I need a distraction from thinking about how I may never find someone to share and make a life with.

Ending up alone is very much in the cards for me, and the idea breaks my heart.

CHAPTER FOUR
SIMON

Don't you dare look out the window again.

I click the volume button on my phone twice. If the music is loud enough, maybe I won't be able to hear myself think about Greer being outside with my kid.

Does it bother me that I'm in here writing while she's out there playing catch? Of fucking course it does. I should be out there. I should be the one he's happily running down the stairs to see, the one who lights up his face after saying yes to him.

Me.

Not anyone else.

My fingers sprint over the keyboard. I need at least another thousand words for today, and then I can call it for the day and send Greer home. Being in Greer's house to let the yard guy in did its job. I didn't snoop, but I did take my time, letting some of my original ideas come back to me before I locked up. It's helped more than she will ever know.

If I weren't so disciplined, I'd skip out right now. But I have commitments, and sticking to the things you say you'll do is something I've been trying to drill in Grey's head. Bailing isn't the example I want to set.

I'm writing a single dad romance; adding in how messy the house gets seems to fit in well right now. Grey isn't wrong on that either. I've been so busy between his summer sports, The Space downtown, and the multiple deals I have going on in my book world, I've let a few things slack off. And I feel guilty because I'm not planning enough time in my day for Grey.

I lean back, my gaze drifting to the window outside. Grey is smiling and running in front of Greer, the ball tucked into his side.

She's hot on his heels, laughing.

Barefoot too. Why can't I let that small detail go?

I don't ever remember football being funny, but whatever game they're playing, I like the way it looks on Grey.

Calla and my mom are the two women he's used to being around. So I'm not too sure how I feel about Greer spending time with him.

Hell, I'm not so sure how I feel being around her myself.

Every part of me seems to come to a full alert stance. I'm aware of how close she's standing to me, how she smells like vanilla mixed with lavender, no matter if she's fresh from the shower or if she's just finished a workout, how she always smiles and has a solution to whatever topic is at hand. It's hard not to notice Greer when she's in the same room as you.

As soon as she went outside with Grey, I cut my workout short so that I could get to writing and call it a day sooner.

It's not lost on me the lack of clothing between her and me on the porch. Me shirtless and her with her skintight gym outfit.

It was yet another moment where I wasn't sure how to feel around Greer. Am I annoyed that her body made me think things it shouldn't or grateful because she's a beautiful woman, and I couldn't take my eyes off her? She wore those clothes like they were made for her.

I sigh and lace my hands behind my head.

I don't think the words are going to happen if all I can think about is the fact that someone else is having fun with Grey.

I save my work, make a few notes for what I want to have in my next scenes, change into a clean shirt, and then head outside.

Grey and Greer are stretching in the grass when I step out.

"Done already?" I ask and glance at my watch. It's only been an hour.

"Just taking a break to stretch," Grey says, and Greer nods a smile. "Really, it's for me. He was winning, and I had to stop that."

Grey laughs. "We should do this on all the days I don't have a camp going. You could come hang out with me while my dad works."

Hell.

"Oh, I'm sure he doesn't work that much."

"He works a lot." He looks at me. "But I know you're just trying to give me a good life, Dad. I'm not sad."

How did I get so lucky with this kid?

And even though I don't say it, he's right. I work a lot. A lot more than I used to.

"How about right now, I take over for Greer?"

"Seriously?" Grey's face lights up, and he jumps to my feet. "Like for real? Not a 'let's play for five minutes and then head inside to clean or cook or do something in the house?'"

I hold back the cringe. He makes me sound like dad of the year, doesn't he?

"Like for real."

He runs to me and gives me a high five as Greer stands behind him.

"I'll let you two get to it."

"Thank you," I say as she passes.

I don't know if it's because of how close she is, the way her eyes lock on mine, or because I've written more heroines with a secret than I can count in my books, but it's clear as day that she's hiding something.

I shouldn't care what it is.

And I sure as hell shouldn't ask her about it.

"Is everything okay?"

She laughs with a small head shake. "Everything is fine. I'll see you two around, and if he ever needs someone to hang out with, my door is open."

I watch her disappear inside, and although I don't believe a word she says, I have a kid waiting for me, and that's my focus right now.

Almost two hours later, we head inside. Dinner and cleaning, as my son called me out for earlier, are calling my name.

"Holy smokes!" Grey says, beating me to the back door. "Look at this place."

I step in behind him and stop in my tracks. The dishes are clean; I hear the sound of the dishwasher running. The trash is gone. I pull out the drawer for it and sure enough, a fresh clean bag is in its place. As I move farther into my house, I notice the neatly folded piles of clothes and the coats hung by the door, shoes lined up underneath them.

There's a sticky note on the back of the front door: Sorry if I overstepped. I hope this gives you a little more time together.

"Sandwiches!" Grey calls from the kitchen and then starts to jog down the hall with one in each hand. "See, I told you an assistant was a good idea. Now we can go to the new Spiderman movie after we eat."

I nod slowly, watching him sit on the couch and devour his turkey sandwich like it's the first one he's ever had.

This feels weird as hell, knowing Greer cleaned my house and made us food. For what? Why would she do this? I'm not a dick, but I know I'm not always the friendliest person there is. At the same time, it's six in the evening, and I can spend the rest of my night doing whatever Grey wants.

I, too, take a bite of my sandwich.

If I had someone to help, just for a little while, I could have more nights like this. With Grey. Less guilt.

Looks like I'm hiring someone to help after all. I just hope Greer's up for the job, because letting a stranger into my house isn't an option.

CHAPTER FIVE
GREER

I didn't get any sleep last night. Instead, I laid in bed, thinking about my actions.

I cleaned his house, folded his clothes, and made them sandwiches.

That's like super creeper status, right?

Who does that?

Me. That's who. A woman who was avoiding another night alone.

I push back into downward dog and pinch my eyes closed. I should have just left his house like I was supposed to.

I let out a breath.

I should apologize on my way home.

I lift my right leg high.

He'll probably slam the door in my face.

I switch legs.

He has every right. I overstepped. I totally overstepped.

A throat clears, and I drop to my knees, looking up to see

Simon standing over me. His arms are crossed, and he has a scowl on his face.

"Hi," I say and slowly stand in front of him. It's not like he's going to lunge at me or even move from where his feet are firmly planted, but I hold my hands in front of me anyway. "I'm sorry I didn't leave yesterday like you asked me to. It was wrong to just help myself to your house, and I'm truly so sorry for that."

He lets out a deep sigh and drops his chin to his chest. Then he adjusts his stance wider and rests his hands on his hips.

This is not a moment where I should be checking Simon out. I do it anyway.

The longer we stand here, and he remains quiet, the worse I feel.

"Simon, I—"

"I'm not mad, Greer," he says, finally looking up. His gaze captures mine like a magnet, and I barely swallow without choking.

"Oh."

"In fact"—he pauses to walk around me and sit on the workbench— "it gave me an entire night with Grey. No responsibilities no… anything but hanging out with my son."

"Ah. Well, I'm glad."

That wasn't my intention, but I'm glad my need for a distraction helped him.

"It also made me realize that right now, I've made more commitments in my career than I care to admit. Commitments that are taking away time with Grey."

I want to say something motivational or give him a hug. Going by the tension in his shoulders, he didn't want to admit what he just said, but honestly, this is the most he's ever said in a conversation, and I'm a little shocked.

"You're a successful author, Simon. You just opened a new business. You work hard, and it shows. It's not a bad example to set."

He nods slowly. "I want to be a successful dad too."

Oh, wow.

I will not cry in front of him, but that was so sweet.

I sit next to him. The bench isn't small, but my leg brushes his wide frame. His attention falls to where we're touching.

"You *are* a good dad, Simon. One of the best I've ever seen."

He looks up into my eyes, and for a split second, I swear his gaze flickers to my lips. But the motion was quick so I'm not sure it happened.

We sit long enough in the silence for my heart to race, for my cheeks to feel flush, and for the urge to kiss him to take over.

I've always been attracted to Simon but wanting to kiss him—that's new.

I clear my throat and stand.

"Anyway, did you need something? You don't normally come in here."

I gesture to my studio space and cross my arms.

"Grey and I talked it over, and we'd like to know if you can help us over the summer."

"Help you how?"

Simon rises to his feet, reaches into his back pocket, and pulls out his phone.

"Grey has football camp three afternoons a week followed by soccer, and a ninja warrior camp the other two days. When he isn't doing that, he's sitting at the house playing video games while he waits for me to finish work. Even then, it's housework and cooking and the list never ends. I'd like to hire you to run him to those camps, help around the house, and hang out with Grey while I work. Then when the day is over, the only thing for me to do is spend time with him."

He lets out a breath, almost like admitting all of that to me took a lot. Which I'm sure it did.

"Oh, like a nanny?"

"Essentially, yes. Grey is self-sufficient. But we could use the help, and I will pay you. Just give me a number."

He steps closer, and his woodsy scent surrounds me.

I take a breath, loving the way he smells.

"I'm not sure that's a good idea."

"Why not?"

"I…" I don't really have a reason.

"Look, I don't trust a lot of people, and Grey likes you."

"Why not ask Calla?"

Simon sighs. "Never mind."

He brushes past me. Do I want to be a nanny? Not really. Do I want a distraction from being alone all the time? Yes.

"Wait," I call out. "I'll come over when I get off work so we can set a schedule. I have clients in the mornings, so I can't be there until around noon each day."

It's faint, but a twitch of a smile tugs at Simon's lips.

"That will work just fine. See you after lunch."

He pushes out the door, leaving me standing here a little in shock at what just happened.

But right now, all I can think about is how, for the next three months, I'm not going home to an empty house where I sit alone.

CHAPTER SIX
SIMON

Summer has always been a strong writing season for me. I swear, there's something about being able to sit outside while I'm writing that makes the words flow easier. I read somewhere being in the sun in general can be just as much of an energy booster as working out. It's a completely different type of endorphins to improve mood.

I believe it.

I feel unstoppable when I write outside.

I let out a breath and lean back.

It could be the sun or the fresh air that has me writing more words today than I have in weeks, but I'm going to assume it has more to do with Greer than anything. To the idea that my life is going to be easier for the remainder of the summer.

I don't like to admit that I need help. Hell, I'm not one for conversation, but being alone with Greer this morning, I shared more with her than I had planned. I can't explain it. I was honestly just going to walk in there and ask her to help, but then… then she'd been doing yoga. I should feel guilty that I spotted her through the front window before I walked in. That I watched her for a moment too long. Long enough for my dick to get an idea it shouldn't. For my mind to go places I really can't afford for it to go.

Fuck.

When she went into downward dog, leaving would have been smart, but Grey likes Greer. My sister likes Greer. All my friends know her. She's the perfect fit for what I need.

So I gave myself a pep talk and walked into her studio and now—now I'm waiting on the porch for her to come home.

I see her before I hear her.

She rounds the corner on her bike, smiling. Her eyes go wide, and she laughs. Then she spots me, rips the headphones from her ears, and comes to a stop.

"Hi, Simon." She kicks her kickstand down and then climbs off the bike. She's changed her clothes, but instead of the plum yoga pants she'd been wearing earlier, she's got on another one of those sport dresses.

Like the one she was wearing for her date and how he let her down that night.

A piece of me wishes I knew who it was.

"No *hi* back? I guess you did talk enough earlier to cover about a week's worth of conversations for us."

I raise a brow as she walks toward me.

The only downfall of this whole thing, aside from the attraction I now have to fight off, is the fact that Greer is never in a bad mood. Hell, a man stood her up the other day, and the next day she brought me cookies and stayed to play football with my kid.

She's cheery.

She's definitely hiding something.

"I thought all three of us could do the afternoon together. This way, you can see our routine."

She nods. "Right to it, huh?"

She shrugs off one strap of her backpack and swings it around to her front so she can grab the drink sitting in one of the side cupholders.

It's a white cup with a straw.

Grey comes barging out of the house.

"Greer! You're here."

"Hey!"

He runs up and hugs her and then points at her cup. "What's that?"

"A chocolate peanut butter and banana protein shake."

"Oh! Can I have one after camp today?"

Greer looks at me. "I don't know. Is that part of the routine?"

"Routine?" Grey laughs. "My dad had to hire you because we don't have one."

"Grey."

One thing's for sure. When Greer is around, my son and I both have a habit of saying a little too much. I'll need to talk to him about that.

"What?"

"We have a routine," I remind him.

"Okay, Dad."

"We do."

"Go get your stuff," I say, and he does as he's told. Once he's inside, I say to Greer, "Don't feel obligated to make him shakes or anything."

"I can if he's allowed to have them. Maybe once a week."

I nod. "We should talk about how much I'm going to pay you."

"Or you cannot, and this is just a friend helping a friend."

I watch her for a moment.

"I'm going to pay you."

"I don't want your money, Simon."

"Then why are you here?"

"Because you need help, and I have the time."

I shake my head.

"No, I'm paying you."

"Well, you'll just have a stack of uncashed checks."

"I'll give you cash."

"Then I'll give it to Grey."

I cross my arms and stand tall. Greer moves her sunglasses to the top of her head and slowly takes me in.

I won't lie—it's like she's looking right through me. Or reading my mind. Like she knows all the dirty things I want to do to her, and the look she's giving me is her permission that she would let me do all those things and more.

Normally, I'd change the subject, but instead, I find myself walking down the steps to meet her on the sidewalk.

"I'll pay you seven hundred a week. That's final."

"Simon," she scolds me.

"Are you going to argue with me about everything I ask?"

She shakes her head. "Only if it's worth arguing."

"Do you want to tell me why you won't take my money?"

"I'm just helping a friend."

I rub my chin, never taking my eyes off her. "A friend."

She grins. "Yep."

"You won't tell me why you don't want my money, and you're just helping a friend. What aren't you telling me?"

She lets out a long breath. "Honestly, right now, I'm considering changing my mind."

She crosses her arms and holds eye contact. A clear challenge. One I can't afford to take part in.

"We'll take my truck, and I'm staying firm on seven hundred."

I pack my bag quickly, taking my computer and things inside, grateful she didn't argue with me again. When I walk back to the driveway, Grey is whispering something to Greer, who's crouched down to his level. She spots me, Grey spins to look at me, and smiles.

"I told her I wanted grilled cheese and tomato soup for dinner."

I don't respond for two reasons. One, I've already told Greer she isn't his maid, and two, yeah, that sounds like a delicious plan to me too.

I open the rear door for Grey and then do the same for Greer with the passenger door before heading around to my own.

We all load up, seat belts on, and are nearly out of the driveway when Grey starts with his questions.

"If you're helping me and my dad, does this mean you don't have a job anymore at your workout place?"

"I work at the studio and with you and your dad."

"But why not work at the studio all day?"

"I work one-on-one with clients, and a lot of them work during the day, so mornings and a few evenings are all I need."

"But won't you be with us in the evenings?"

"Yes. Right now, I have two evening clients. I thought

maybe you could come with me on those nights and join us if you want."

"Like working out with a real personal trainer?"

"Yes."

"Sweet! That's so cool. Thanks, Greer."

"Anytime."

I don't speak during my son's interrogation, because these are all questions I would ask myself once Grey was on the field.

"What did you normally do during the day?" Grey asks as if it were an afterthought.

"Oh, this and that. Hang out."

"Who do you hang out with? Most of the people I know work during the day?"

Greer doesn't answer right away, so I sneak a glance her way. Her focus is out the window as we pass through downtown to get to the event fields.

"I usually hang out alone."

Her answer is soft and quick.

"Oh, that sucks. Sometimes, I wish I had more alone time, but Dad is always around. Now I'll have you, and that's pretty exciting."

"Hey, I like hanging out with you," I told him.

"I like hanging out with you, too, but I'm getting older, and I need space."

Greer lets out the smallest of laughs. "Oh, you do know how to smile," she says and points at me. "Not bad."

Is she flirting with me?

The fields appear before I can think much of it. Grey is racing to meet his friends as soon as he's out of the truck.

"So, I park, and he runs off. It's a good thing you drove us here to show me the ropes."

She grabs the bag from my hand and waits for me to get the rest of Grey's stuff.

I pull out a soft cooler and sling the strap over my shoulder, ignoring her teasing tone.

"Today was our day to bring snacks. The moms"—I nod toward the bleachers— "will not let you forget when it's your turn."

"Noted."

"They'll probably talk your ear off too."

I lock the truck, and we head toward the other parents.

"I love my kid, but I won't miss sitting here answering question after question from them."

"Oh, I'm sure it's not that bad."

"Simon, yoo-hoo!"

"Hi, Simon."

The closer we get, the more moms say hi.

"Afternoon ladies, this is Greer. She'll be bringing Grey to camp for the summer."

I take a seat; Greer plants herself right between me and the other moms.

"Hi," she says with a smile and a wave.

"Oh no. We love having you here."

A few more moms say something similar before I have a moment to respond. Greer turns her head to me. She's biting her bottom lip as if it's going to help contain the smile on her face. I'm not sure which one distracts me more.

Or maybe it's how close she is, or maybe it's when she leans in and her scent surrounds me, but right here, right now,

I have to remember one thing: Greer is doing me a favor, and I should not screw it up by making a move on her.

But hell, those lips. The things I would love to see them do.

"I don't think they'll be chatting my ear off," she says quietly. "It's *you* they want to talk to." She nudges my hips.

It was a simple poke, but my body reacts like some lovesick high school boy.

I turn to the field just as all the boys run out to scrimmage.

Hiring the first woman my body has reacted to in years may not have been the best plan.

CHAPTER SEVEN
GREER

For as long as I can remember, taking care of myself and others has been what I love to do. Whether it's physical or emotional, I want to do the best that I can.

I sip my smoothie and review today's calendar. I have two more clients before I head off to Simon's to grab Grey.

I smile to myself.

Those moms loved Simon. When I show up tomorrow, there's no doubt in my mind that I'll get a stink-eye or two, but who can blame them? Simon is this mysterious dad. I'm sure they're all wondering why he isn't dating, why a man who looks like him has never been married. I didn't look close enough to see if all of them were married, but I'm sure if there was a single one, she would have made a move by now.

But once they get a real dose of the grumpy ole Simon, I bet they'd be singing a different tune.

"Morning," Willa says, popping into the back of the studio from our connecting door.

"Good morning," I reply as she takes a seat across from me. "Busy day?"

"A little." She grabs her phone. "Natalie Miller is coming in today. She's been wanting to check out my meal plans, and she asked if you had any openings."

"Oh, I love that. Natalie is so sweet. It would be nice to know her a little better."

Since joining Willa's group of friends a couple of years ago, I've met Natalie a handful of times. She spends a lot of time with her boyfriend these days, though. So I don't think anyone sees her as much as they used to.

"Me too."

"Hello, anybody here?" Calla calls out, appearing from behind me as well. She strolls in with a big smile and a tray of coffees from Love's a Brewing, her sister-in-law's coffee shop. "I brought coffee."

She sets the tray down and rolls one of my workout balls over to sit.

Seeing as this side of the company is for working out, and I typically have only one client at a time, seating is limited. Which, I'm sure, is why she went to Willa's side first.

"To what do we owe this pleasure?" Willa asks.

"I have a super busy day today and thought I'd stop in to see my friends before the chaos began."

"Aww, I know we hardly see each other these days. Where even does the time go?" I ask.

"Tell me about it," Willa agrees. "I have full days and then Zane wants all my free time," she says like it's a hardship, but the smile on her face claims otherwise.

"Same." Calla giggles and points at me with her bagel.

"You have the most free time of all of us. Tell us what it's like."

I smile but a part of my chest aches. Being alone isn't as glamorous as everyone makes it out to be. Yes, it's important, but it's lonely.

"Actually," I say, "I have a little part-time gig to keep me busy until school starts."

"What? Since when?" Willa asks.

"Since yesterday morning."

"Well, what is it?" Calla pries.

"I'm actually helping your brother and Grey."

She studies me for a minute and then nods. "Good. He needs it. He's missed two dinners at our mom's in the last month, all because he can't keep his schedule straight. Or maybe it's because she constantly asks him when he's going to start dating again, but probably mostly because he's busy."

"That's what I'm here for."

"Are you still on those dating apps?" Willa asks. "Sorry I changed that subject so quickly. I just remembered that I saw an ad last night for this documentary about a lady who was murdered meeting a blind date, and I wanted to tell you that I think you need to start giving me"—she points at Calla— "or her the name and address before you meet someone. Even if it's a lunch date. Murderers don't care what time of day it is."

Calla lets out a hoot. "That's the biggest subject change in the history of subject changes."

"I didn't want to forget."

"No worries, Wills. I'm taking a break from the apps until further notice. It's a big reason why I'm helping your brother. I need the distraction. All the available guys out there are just... weird. Dating in your thirties is nothing like dating in your twenties. I swear, the women are ready to settle, and the men are just looking for fun."

"Oh, Greer. I'm sorry. So you're not going to date? And you're exactly thirty. So it should basically be the same thing as last year."

"I'm still going to date. I'm just not going to use an app to meet someone. I tried it. It failed. When it comes down to it, I want that first click moment to be in person. Not because some guy swiped the right way on my profile picture."

"Maybe you should take a break?" Willa suggests.

I've considered it, but all that would do is take me away from my goal, and I don't want that. Finding a different way to reach it—now that sounds more like me.

"Or this is that moment." Calla beams. "You know, where you swear off men, and boom! The right one just appears out of thin air."

"Have you been plotting with Beck again?" Willa asks.

"A little."

"It shows."

"Well, it could happen. I'm the perfect example of how Mr. Right could be right in front of you, and you have no idea till he's gone."

"Considering the only men in my life are your fiancés and husbands, I'm going to say that's not the case here. And I'm not swearing off men, just dating apps."

"And Simon." Willa smiles.

"What?" I ask.

Willa points at me with her coffee. "The only men in your life are husbands, fiancés, and Simon."

"Grumpy Simon?" I ask. "I'm pretty sure Grey made him ask me for help."

"You're probably right there," Calla says. "But I don't mean my brother. As awesome as that would be, I'm afraid he fits the profile of the men in your dating app. He just wants fun. He swears he'll never settle down again. A broken heart is hard to mend, and I just don't think his ever did."

"This is a really depressing coffee break," Willa says.

Calla goes back to eating her breakfast, and I let her words soak in. I never intended to date Simon. Stare at him from time to time, yes. Maybe flirt, yeah, but date? No. Still, her last comment hits me in the heart.

What must it feel like to know you'll end up alone and be okay with it?

Maybe I'll get more from hanging out with him than I think. Maybe I could ask him about how he's come to accept being alone.

Then again, that might include the two of us having to share more personal details than either of us wants.

I sip my coffee.

I never expected to feel empathy like this for Simon.

It makes me want to hug him.

"Okay, I can't dawdle. I need to get going." Calla stands quickly and grabs her things.

"Me too. My first client should be here soon," Willa says.

I give them both a quick hug and start my day.

Grey leads the way when we get to ninja warrior camp held at Wind Valley's recreation center. It's a special room set up with various obstacle courses, and as soon as he makes it into the classroom, I take a seat outside of it to watch through the viewing window.

Ninja warrior camp.

Ha.

I love that they're coming up with more and more ideas to keep kids busy, but this is something I would have never imagined. But truth be told, if there had been a ninja warrior camp when I was a kid, I would have gone.

The kids line up on a bench inside the room as a man slowly paces in front of them. He's obviously the teacher and is giving them some kind of instruction.

He's tall—my guess is a little over six feet. He has dark hair that's cut short and clean, and his face is clear of any facial hair. From the way his black slacks hang on his hips and his black T-shirt clings to his biceps, he's clearly fit. Then he turns, and I see his dark eyes. One thought crosses my mind. He's my type. A 100 percent my type.

Is it possible that on day one of no dating apps, I could actually meet someone organically? I try to sneak a peek at his left hand, but he keeps it hidden. What are the chances he's single?

I sigh and look at my phone, checking my schedule for tomorrow. Grey's coach is probably not the smartest idea anyway. I'd have to see him all summer if things didn't work out.

Do I really have room to be picky?

A text from Calla comes up in the group chat I have with her, Willa, and one of our newest friends, Paige.

CALLA

I was thinking about this morning, and I feel like we should have addressed your dating subject more.

WILLA

I agree. I actually came up with an idea. Do you remember when Paige told us about her bucket list?

GREER

Yes.

PAIGE

Oh, I see it. Greer should make a list.

WILLA

Yes! If all the guys you've been dating keep having the same result, maybe make a list of what you want in a partner. That way, you can stop wasting time with the ones who don't meet the criteria.

It's not a bad idea. I mean, I have a basic idea in my head, but they might be onto something. Maybe the kind of man I'm attracted to isn't the type of man I should end up with. I'm still on the no-dating band wagon, but perhaps they didn't work out because I haven't been clear on what I want in a man.

GREER

It's worth a try.

I pull up the notes app, and my thumb hovers over what to type. Before I can get the chance to start my list, my phone buzzes again, only this time it's from Simon.

SIMON

How's it going?

GREER

The whole five minutes we've been here?

The text bubbles pending his response appear. When a message doesn't come through, I lean back and send another.

GREER

It's good. He's still in one piece. I sort of wish they had this for me as a kid.

SIMON

Good. See you at home.

No response to my casual conversation? Makes sense, considering I'm only here so that he can get more work done. If he wanted to chat, he'd be here instead of me.

Grey waves at me through the glass, and I wave back.

Simon said he wanted to be a successful dad. I don't spend a lot of time with him or Grey, not yet anyway, but I can already tell that he is.

Maybe I can find a way to show him that while I'm helping.

I pull the notes app back up and stare at the blank screen. I could just start the list with the typical *kind, thoughtful, likes conversation* gooey stuff, but heck, past that, I don't know what to list. I just want someone who wants what I want.

Is it because I have this need to have everything my mom didn't have while I was growing up? I think she was happy, but I always wondered, if she had someone to share her life with romantically after my dad died, would she have been happier?

Do I think it'll make me happier?

I spend the next hour flipping back and forth from my planner to my list, and before I know it, the door to Grey's class opens and one by one, the kids exit and meet their parents. Grey is the last one, and he's walking out with his instructor.

"Greer!" Grey beams. "This is Mr. Remy."

His smile spreads wide as he stretches a hand to me, his eyes practically glowing when they land on mine.

"Hi, it's a pleasure to meet you. You can call me Calvin. Grey talked about you nonstop all through class."

"What? She's really cool."

"I take that as a sign he only said good things."

Calvin nods. "Very kind things."

I ruffle Grey's hair. "Now I'm curious."

"I'm going to go get my other shoes. I'll be back." Grey runs off, leaving Calvin and me alone.

"He's a great kid. He has a lot of spirit, and he learns quickly."

"Yes, he's almost too smart and wise for his age, but don't tell him I said that."

Calvin laughs, and it's a deep laugh that makes my smile grow bigger.

Grey is back in a flash, clearly ready to head out as he starts for the exit.

"I'll see you around," I say quickly and follow Grey.

"You can bet on it," Calvin says and waves.

I leave the gym with a giddiness I haven't felt in a while. But the thought remains that dating one of Grey's coaches might not be a good idea.

I mean, I'm not ruling it out. Not yet.

After all, maybe it's as a simple as Calla said earlier. Mr. Right could be right in front of me, and I don't even know it.

CHAPTER EIGHT
SIMON

I added more items to my to-do list than I crossed off. How is that possible?

Today was the first day for me to make progress without interruption, and all I did was add to the mess.

I skim my current work in progress. My current scene is boring. I'm bored. I need to think of something new. I don't even want to write it, which means a reader won't want to read it. It's officially a did-not-finish chapter.

I sigh, leaning back in my chair and twisting my cap backward. I rub my eyes with my palms just as my phone rings.

I don't normally keep the volume on, but for the last hour, I've been going back and forth with my agent on the ending of my previous book. Although I'm grateful for his help, I don't like the direction he wants me to go.

And that's exactly why I answered his call with my opinion.

"I don't want him to die," I say in a tone that leaves no room for further discussion.

I put my phone on speaker as I await his reply.

Yes, I want to write what the readers want, but what good is that book if I don't like it more?

"Then you need a new ending. If he dies, this book will be talked about on every media outlet," Doug says louder than I'd planned.

I turn the volume down a notch and shake my head as if he could see me.

"Yeah, they'll all be talking about how they don't want to read my books anymore if I plan to kill off a beloved character."

"You need something to shock them."

"Well, someone else has to die," I say, just as I hear the front door squeak open or closed again. Whatever Greer and Grey are doing, they've been going in and out for the last hour. As soon as they came home this afternoon, I almost called it a day, but the whole point is for Greer to help me get caught up and get ahead. I have to make it work. The sooner I'm caught up, the sooner I can spend more time with Grey and prioritize better.

I should have figured this out sooner.

"Who else could you kill to give them the plot twist they need?"

"Does anyone have to die?"

"Yes."

"Why not make the sister the murderer? She has access to the house and everything around them."

"That makes no sense."

"Hence the plot twist."

"What's her reasoning?"

"Love. Duh. She wants the husband for herself. Maybe she has a shrine."

Doug laughs, and it makes me smile because this volley of working out a plot issue is one of my favorite parts of the writing process.

"Write me the chapters, and I'll let you know my thoughts."

"You got it."

"Okay, I'm going to go eat dinner with my wife now. I'm surprised you're still working. Don't you usually only work a couple hours a day these days?"

I sigh, glancing at the clock to see it's just after six.

He's right. I should get upstairs. Greer and I didn't exactly talk about her hours, and this might be abusing it.

"I have a nanny now. Well, nanny-ish. One of Calla's friends is helping me out for the summer so I can meet deadlines and Grey can still go to all his camps."

"Oh, that's good news. So I can expect to see your work by the end of the week."

I laugh. He's one of the main people who gets my working late because I can't keep my to-do list straight.

"I have a good feeling that will happen."

"Good. Now, have a good night."

"You too."

I end the call, glancing at my office door when I hear the squeak again.

What the hell are they up to?

I close my computer and scoot in my chair. When I step into the main room of the basement, I move to the bookshelf in the corner that opens to my very own library.

Grey knows about this room, but to everyone else, it's just a bookshelf in the basement. Last summer when my basement flooded, I'd intended to remodel the basement the same way it was, but then Calla didn't move back in, so I decided to add this piece for myself in the main room. The shelf directly across from this one opens to a little hideaway for Grey. We went all out to make it what we wanted. Big main room, office, secret rooms, and a gym in what should have been the spare room. I'd say we didn't miss a beat.

While his space is smaller and has a TV and gaming set, mine is floor-to-ceiling bookshelves everywhere but one wall. That wall has photos of my bestselling books, and a reading chair. I do a lot of final edits in that chair.

Every book I've written since I put that room in has become a bestseller. Maybe that's why no one knows about it.

I secure the shelf before jogging up the stairs.

As soon as I reach the top of the stairs, the smell of something baking swallows me, and I have to pause to inhale.

Fuck. That smells like heaven.

I can't pinpoint exactly what it is, but it's a home-cooked meal. It's not takeout or delivered pizza again, and for that I am glad. It's also not a meal I've cooked before. I've never smelled something this good. Something that makes my stomach growl before it even knows what it is.

As soon as I'm finished obsessing over the smell of dinner, I move into the living room. Again, I pause. It's so clean.

I move farther into the room and swipe a finger on the fireplace mantel.

Not a speck of dust.

I let out a breath. For as much as it pained me not to take over when I heard Greer and Grey come home, I didn't realize how thankful I'd be to have her here. It's only day one, and I can already tell that Greer is going to lower my stress level more than I imagined.

Grey's laughter steals my attention from the room. I move to the kitchen, groaning at the heavenly smell I wish I could just devour right this second, and open the back door to see Grey and Greer tossing the football back and forth.

This makes me feel like a horrible parent. The guilt over wanting my career to be successful consumes me. I should be the one playing with him.

I have a job where I make my own hours. I should have changed my schedule years ago. Still, as it is, I have so much on my plate that unless I chose to have three- or four-hour sleep nights, I'd never get it done.

Greer is a good thing. This was the right choice. I just need to accept it, no matter how hard it may be.

"Dad!" Grey shouts as he catches the ball. He runs toward me with a big smile. That right there makes all this worth it. If he's happy, so am I.

"Hey, bud, how was camp?"

"It was great. I learned some new moves today."

He jumps into the air and then pretends to kick me while I fake how hard he hit me.

"You'll have to show them to me later," I say, ruffling his hair.

He swats my hand away.

"After we eat," he says and pushes through the door. "We were waiting for you, and I'm starrrrving."

He disappears into the kitchen just as Greer steps onto the patio.

"What was your favorite scene to write today?"

She pauses in front of me as if she's genuinely interested in what I did today. Her eyes focus on mine as she waits for a reply.

Outside of my agent and the guys, I can't remember the last time someone asked me about my writing. My family used to ask me. I know they care, but maybe they think that after so many books, I'm less excited about a new one. Which, of course, is never the case. Readers, sure, they ask about the next book, but something about the way Greer asked this simplest question—it's different.

"Was that too personal? I know writers like to keep things private till a book is finished. I hope I didn't overstep. I just think it's really cool that you—"

"No, that's not it. It just threw me off that that was the first topic you chose to discuss."

"Oh." She looks into the kitchen and then back at me as if she isn't sure she'll keep standing here. "Still, just tell me if you'd rather not talk about it."

"Okay."

That's all I can say. Of all the words in the world, *okay* is the one I chose to go with.

"Okay," she repeats and then steps into the kitchen.

What did I expect? For her to stand there and wait for me to think of something to say?

"Finally," Grey says. He's unwrapping a dish with some type of salad in it. He's already pulled plates and silverware and napkins and placed them on the table.

I notice it right away: three spots.

Greer must notice at the same time.

"Oh, that's so sweet, Grey, but I'm not staying for dinner."

"What? Why not? You cooked all this food."

He's not wrong. I know what her role is and so does she, but it never occurred to me that she'd be cooking our dinner just to go home and cook her own. It would make sense for her to stay and eat with us.

She nods and casts a quick glance in my direction before she looks back at Grey.

"Yes, but my job is done now, and I have food at home waiting for me."

Grey's face says exactly what I'm thinking. The thing is, I'm not sure why I'm so bothered by it. Greer has never eaten dinner with us outside of that one dinner to discuss Grey's meal plans.

"You should stay," I blurt out without thinking.

"Yeah!" Grey chimes in.

Greer looks between us, her hair shining from the early evening sun beaming through the window and her eyes lighting up as she smiles.

"That's really sweet, but I can't."

She holds her hand up for Grey to high-five.

"But I'll be back tomorrow, and when we get to football camp, you can show them all how good your arm got in just one day. If you want to be a quarterback, I think you can do it."

"Quarterback?" I ask. "I didn't know you picked a position."

Grey nods proudly as Greer heads for the front door.

"Dish up. I'll be right back," I say to Grey and then follow her.

"Greer, wait up," I call out.

She doesn't stop until she's at the door.

She grabs her purse, lifting it over her shoulder to cross over her body. Instantly, my eyes fall to where it dips between her breasts, making them stand out.

I pull myself together before she can notice, then grab onto the doorframe, both hands resting above us as I ask, "Are you sure you can't stay?"

The smile she gives me is small and sweet.

"Not tonight."

"Do you have other plans?" I have no idea why I pushed back. If she has other plans, that's fine.

It's because she told Grey she couldn't stay. That's it. I hate when my kid doesn't get what he wants.

"Goodnight, Simon," she says and walks out the door.

When she's off the front porch, she looks over her shoulder. Her eyes lock on mine as she bites her bottom lip.

Oh, hell.

She turns back to cross the grass.

"Greer." I open the door.

I wait for her to look back. "I decided to add a love triangle to my book today. It's new for me."

She crosses her arms and nods with a grin.

"If anyone can do it, it's Simon Stone."

With that, she jogs the rest of the way to her house and disappears inside.

I'm still standing on my porch, looking at her house, when Grey calls my name from the kitchen.

Does Greer read my books?

If she does, does she like them?

Does she think I'm a good writer?

I head back into the house and join Grey at the table.

"Why are you smiling like that?" he asks.

I can't help it—I laugh at his question.

If I had an answer, I'd tell him.

All I know is that today was a good day, and I can't wait to see Greer tomorrow.

CHAPTER NINE
GREER

How long can a person sit and stare at their new car?

How long is too long?

I rock back on one of the chairs on Simon's front porch the way I have every day for the past week after Grey and I come back from whatever camp he had that day. Only this time, I can't take my eyes off my brand-new slate-blue Bronco.

I smile, but it's a sad smile.

Growing up, my mother worked two jobs to give me everything I wanted. I wasn't a needy kid by any means, and I was well aware of the situation we were in, so I didn't cry or fight her when she said no. All I knew was that one day, I'd make sure I worked as hard as she did for my family.

She would be so proud of how far I've come. I wish she were here so I could tell her that my work ethic came from her. She's the reason I set goals and have my own house, a job I love, and a car I bought all on my own.

I'm doing the damn thing, making my dreams happen,

but… I don't have a family to share it with. That one person I get to come home to. The person I share everything with, celebrating something as silly as a new car.

One day.

I hope.

I let out a breath and glance at Grey, who's writing in a new journal. He asked me earlier about journaling his workouts and what he eats. He wants to pinpoint what it is that makes him feel better on some days and less on others. Who am I to say no to someone who wants to better themselves? So what that he's a kid, or that by next week he could move on to the next hot trend? Telling him no is hard.

He must sense me watching because he looks up.

"What?" He laughs.

"Nothing. How's the journal coming?"

"Umm"—he leans back— "a lot less fun than I thought it would be."

I laugh and move to sit by him.

"This may not be the right thing to say, but it's something my mom once told me. If it's not working or you don't like it, stop and move on. Never quit—just move on to finding what does work."

Huh, sounds like my dating life.

"So if I decide this sucks, you won't be mad at me?"

"Why would I be mad?"

"You keep a journal, right?"

"I used to." I tap my temple. "But I store it all up here now. I never stopped; I just found a better way to help myself."

"I think I might be that kind of person too. Dad writes everything down. I hope he's okay with me not doing that."

I give him a side hug and squeeze. "As long as you're happy, he's happy. I promise."

"Can I ask you something?" Grey says, leaning back and crossing his arms. The look he gives me is very serious for a ten-year-old.

"Yes."

"What do you think of my dad?"

I let out a small laugh." What?"

"My dad. Do you like him?"

"Of course. I work for him, don't I?"

"Not like that. I mean like a crush."

"Ah." I instantly spot the way his fingers twist together. "Why do you ask?"

"I just… there's this girl. She's one of my friend's twins."

Oh my god. He has a crush. This is too cute. Oh wow. Has he told Simon?

I do my best to hold back my grin and the giddy tease I want to give him, and I simply nod.

"Okay, what does this have to do with me and your dad?"

"Well, you two are always doing this long stare thing when you talk. I do that with her. Does that mean she likes me too?"

Long stare thing. What is he talking about?

"I'm not sure I know what you mean, but the only sure way to know is to ask her."

He nods.

"I'm not so sure Kev would like that. I guess I could ask him."

At ten, there are so many things happening. Girls are one of them, and although I could give him the traditional "there are better things to focus on" talk, I don't. I'm not his mom or his dad. I'm his friend.

"Do you want to tell me about her?"

He blushes. He actually bushes, and oh my god, I want to gush so freaking bad. I can't wait to talk to Simon about this.

"Have you told your dad?"

"No way. He'd tell me to focus on football or school or something."

"I can't argue with that."

"I want my dad to like you," he says softly. "He's different when you're around. He's always a good dad, but when you're here, it's like… he's more… fun. Happy."

"Oh, I'm sure—"

Simon's truck pulls into the driveway.

"See, right there," Grey beams. "Look at his face. He can't stop looking at you, and he's probably not even in park yet."

Simon is staring right at us. My heart races a little at the thought of seeing him tonight.

Every night since that first one, he walks me to the door when I leave, and he tells me goodbye while hanging on it and grinning at me. I never thought a pose would be such a turn-on. And every night when he does sit, I try not to watch as he flips his cap backward before reaching for the trim, his bicep a beacon for my eyes. And every night, I go home wishing I'd met him at a different time in life. It would make this so-called crush that Grey just called me out for a whole less painful.

"I think he's looking at *us,* not just me."

"No, he's not."

I ruffle his hair, and he swats my arms away the same way he does to his dad.

"Go wash up for dinner," I say. He jumps up, taking his journal but stopping at the door.

"Greer."

"Yeah?"

"For the record, I'd be okay if you liked him back."

I don't get much time to dwell on his words before Simon is in front of me. He peeks inside, and then his gaze lands on me. He lets it linger a little too long before he says anything.

That must be the look Grey was talking about.

"How was your day?" he finally asks.

"Good. Nothing too exciting. Work. Camp. Clean. Cook."

He makes a humming noise then sits next to me.

"What were you two laughing about?"

"Oh, nothing. What was your favorite thing to write today?" I ask.

His gaze slides to mine. Slowly, he takes me in from head to toe, and by the time he's looking into my eyes again, I swear my breathing has picked up.

"Do you really want to know?"

I swallow, nodding, but before he can tell me, I change the subject.

"Grey has a crush on one of his friend's sisters. Honestly, I don't think I should have just told you that, but he was so cute." I slap a hand to Simon's thigh and wiggle it as I let out the tiniest of squeals. "You should have seen his eyes when he mentioned her. It was adorable."

His first crush. Heartbreak sucks, but there's just something about those first moments that can't ever be taken away. When your palms sweat or your heart races or your mouth goes dry. The nervousness and excitement that come with the thought of starting something new just can't be beat.

I lean back, ready to wait for Simon to respond. I'm taking his silence as he doesn't think this is as exciting as I do, but as my body moves back, my hand slides up his thigh, and I don't miss the deep inhale he makes right before I remove my hand.

"I'm sorry," I say quickly. "I didn't notice I did that."

His head bobs a moment.

"It's fine."

His chest rises with each breath. I'm not so sure he's as fine as he says he is.

"Are you sure? I think I made you uncomfortable, and I'm truly sorry."

He stands abruptly. "I'm fine, Greer. Trust me."

"Okay," I say without question. I might not believe him, but if I push it, I'll just make it awkward, and I don't want more of that.

I push to stand as well.

"I'll just get my things."

I disappear into the house, leaving him alone on the porch. My bags were already packed from earlier. I've been bringing my purse and a tote each day so that I can work while I wait for Grey at his camps.

With both bags over my left shoulder, I push the front door open only to stumble because it's the same moment Simon chooses to open it.

His hands fall to my hips to steady me. It helps in the fact that I don't fall on my face, but I still manage to smash into him. My chest to his and my cheek flush to his.

"Sorry," I say and push off only for my bag to slip from my shoulder, pulling my shirt with it and half exposing my black lace bra.

The moment I spot my bra showing, my gaze flashes to

Simon to see if he caught it too. Sure enough, he's not looking anywhere else.

He licks his lips, then his gaze meets mine.

And like I just mentioned, my heart starts to race, and my mouth goes dry.

The timer in the kitchen buzzes.

"Oh, shoot!" I drop my bags, breaking whatever spell has begun to take place in the doorway of Simon's house.

I rush down the hall and pull dinner out of the oven.

Simon steps into the space, and I don't have to look at him to know that whatever tension was beginning to form in the other room has followed us into this one.

I set the chicken rice and broccoli casserole on the counter and chance a glance at Simon.

He isn't trying to hide his intensity.

Maybe this is the look Grey was talking about?

To be honest, Simon could either be really mad right now or extremely turned on. I hope it's the latter. At the same time, I hope it's not. Thinking of my neighbor and best friend's brother as anything other than the grumpy guy who lives next door with the cute kid is a bad, bad idea.

Bad.

He steps toward me.

But he's… never been hard on the eyes, and right now, I can't remember the last time I was this nervous with a guy.

"Five minutes," I blurt out and back up, bumping into the refrigerator. "Give it five minutes to cool, and then you can eat."

He keeps moving toward me, and I think he's going to lean in and kiss me… I mean, hell, the slow stalk, never taking his eyes off me—it all screams *he's going to kiss you.*

But no, he just reaches around me to open the fridge and pull out a vitamin water.

"I can wait five minutes," he says and winks at me.

What the heck?

"Oh, it smells so good in here," Grey says, walking in with a big smile. "Are you actually going to stay this time, Greer?"

"I can't." I totally could, but not after whatever the hell just happened with Simon. Can one touch, maybe two, and my little lace reveal really put that much tension between two people?

"You should stay," Simon says, pulling plates from the cabinet.

"I should not," I reply and clap my hands. "I'll see you both tomorrow."

"Night, Greer!" Grey calls as I head out the front. I grab my bags off the floor and then book it from the house without looking back. I'm not letting the doorway thing happen tonight—no siree, I am not.

I'm almost at my front door.

"Greer," Simon calls. This time, he's on the corner of his porch, arms crossed as he leans against it.

Jesus. I have been helping him for one week. One week. Why is this happening to me?

"Did you get a new car?" he asks after I don't say anything.

The question, however, makes me smile and relax. I nod with pride.

"I sure did."

"I like it. Maybe next week you can take Grey and me on a drive, and we can treat you to dinner to celebrate."

"Really?"

"Of course. See you tomorrow."

"Bye."

He gives me one last wave before he steps into his house.

I do the same, dropping to sit on my sofa in a daze.

Oh my god.

Oh. My. God.

I don't have a so-called crush, no. I'm full-on crushing on Simon Stone.

CHAPTER TEN
SIMON

I've been outside for an hour and have written a whole three sentences. Which I've deleted and rewritten about six times. I know the scene and what needs to happen, but my focus is on the house next door, not the words on my screen.

I haven't seen Greer since Friday night. It's Sunday morning now. A whole day without Greer and hell, I know I'm here just waiting to catch a glimpse of her. All it took was five days of her being at my house for me to get comfortable with it. For me to want more of it.

Maybe I just like having her around because it's different from what Grey and I are used to.

A man on his bike rides by, catching my eye, but of course, I think it's Greer, so I look at her house once again.

I sigh and lean back.

I shouldn't like Greer, but it's clear I do. Very fucking clear. At this point, there's no way she can't know that I'm attracted to her.

I know her. I know her better than I should. Even before

she was working for me, Calla would talk about her. Greer wants to get married and have kids. She wants the whole shebang. House, kids, big Christmas, birthdays with balloon banners, and family photos lining the walls in her entryway.

I get it.

As a man who likes his life the way it is, wanting her is not a smart idea. Doing anything about it is also not a smart idea, and yet, on Friday night, I was so close. Too close. I just wanted a taste. Hell, she touched my thigh. No, she gripped my thigh, squeezed it, and I swear flashes of all the things that grip in other places took over: Greer gripping the sheets as I thrust into her, gripping my hair as I lick her core, gripping my cock until I whisper her name in her ear. It was a five-second span, but yeah, all those scenarios crossed my mind.

It didn't help that she asked what I wrote that day. I was at the stage of my writing where I needed to knock out the word count, and my go-to is always to write a sex scene on those days. So I couldn't help but think of how she'd react if I told her. Would she like it? I want her to like it. I'm not afraid to admit that I want to impress Greer. I don't need approval, but knowing how my books might make her feel interests me.

I've heard of readers making comments about reading certain scenes with one hand. It makes me both cringe and grin at the fact I did my job right. What does Greer think when she reads those scenes?

I clear my throat just as Tobias's truck pulls up in front of my house. I wasn't expecting him, so I shut my computer and stand.

He rounds the front of his truck.

"Working on a Sunday?"

Was I? Or was I pretending just so that I could catch Greer?

"A little," I say and nod to his truck. "Early morning drive? I'm only out here because Grey is still crashed in bed."

"It's just after eight. I thought I'd grab a coffee and stop by."

I cross my arms and study him. He's fidgety, and he's not even holding a coffee cup.

I lift my mug. "Want me to go grab you a cup?"

He sighs, clearly distracted. "Sure, I'll wait here."

He sits, dropping his head and rubbing his neck.

I hurry because it's obvious he needs to talk.

I pour his cup and then grab my phone to see a text from Zane.

It's a screenshot of our friend, but more importantly, Tobias's best friend, Natalie's last Instagram post.

It's a picture of her left hand with a square diamond on her ring finger. The caption doesn't have any words. It's just a diamond ring emoji.

I sigh. Now I know why Tobias is here. The thing is though, he's been in such denial about his feelings for his best friend for years that I can't help but wonder if he knows why he's here.

As I head back to the front, I pause at the bottom of the steps to listen for Grey. Silence. That kid would sleep till lunch if I let him.

I rejoin Tobias, sitting across from him.

"So, what's up?"

He nods. "Just hanging out. How's your weekend?"

"So far, so good."

"How is the nanny working out?"

"Good," I say just as I see her round the corner, jogging toward me.

How long has she been out here? I assumed she hadn't left yet. I've been out here for more than an hour.

Shit.

My eyes follow her every stride. All she's doing is running, and I'm mesmerized by her. By the way her ponytail swings, the sweat shining off her face, the crop top that shows her stomach, the—

"Really good, I see," Tobias cuts into my thoughts with a low chuckle. "Clearly, you're into her."

"Yeah," I say without even trying to deny it.

"Are you going to tell her or just stare at her?"

"Probably the latter." I drink my coffee. "There are too many factors why we don't make sense."

"Sure. Hey, Greer!" he calls out, and she stops right in front of us, jogging in place on the sidewalk.

She should just stop moving. Stop bouncing, to be more specific.

Has it really been so long since I've been with a woman that I can't just see her as any other woman trying to get a workout in?

She pulls her headphones out of her ears and then taps her watch before smiling at us.

Of course I can't. This isn't just any woman. This is Greer. The first woman I've been interested in more than just one night with since Grey's mom.

I'm not so sure how to feel about that.

"Good morning, Tobias. You're here early."

He holds up his mug. "Coffee with a friend. Care to join us?"

Her gaze flashes to me, as if she's waiting for me to give her permission.

"I'll get you a cup," I say.

"Okay, let me go grab my shake real quick, and I'll be back."

She jogs the rest of the way to her house, and yes, my eyes follow her.

Those tiny running shorts. Damn. I love them and hate them at the same time.

"Take a quick, cold shower," Tobias says quietly.

Instead of replying, I punch his arm.

"Ouch, fuck," he says, rubbing his bicep. But his smile fades as he says, "It's okay to like someone again—you know that, right?"

I glance to Greer's house, letting Tobais's words sink in. Then I nod.

"It's been eight years, Simon. I didn't know Blair the way you did, but she loved you, man, and my guess is, she'd want you to be happy again. To love again."

"Yeah. I know."

It doesn't hurt to talk about Blair, Grey's mom. In fact, I enjoy it. And Tobias isn't wrong. But the truth is, losing her fucking hurt. Grey wasn't old enough to understand, but it crushed me. I can't ever imagine going through that again. Loving someone and losing them. That's a pain I would never wish on even my worst enemy.

I dip into the house to get Greer her cup of coffee before she comes back. I'm just putting the pot back on the burner when a text comes in from Zane.

Good morning, have you talked to Tobias today?

Before I answer, an idea occurs to me.

Tobias may not want to talk about whatever is bothering him, but the least I can do is distract him for the day. At the same time, I know Greer and I can't be anything more than friends, but that won't stop me from spending more time with her.

Lust isn't the same thing as love, and as long as lust is all there is between us, what's the worst that could happen?

When I hear her voice out front, I shoot a text to Zane and open the screen door.

"Are you two busy today?"

Greer tilts her head and gives me a half smile. "Why?"

"Yeah, why?" Tobias mimics her.

"I know I said let's get dinner to celebrate your new car, but I think we should all go to the lake for the day. Sandy Beach is calling my name." I nod to her Bronco. "We can put the top down."

Her smile makes all the back and forth in my mind over what I should do about Greer disappear.

"I'm in."

"Me too," Tobias says. "Should I bring the boat, or do you want a full-on beach day?"

"Beach day," Greer answers first. "Grey will love playing football in the sand."

Of course, a day to celebrate her turns into her thinking of my kid first.

Lust, not love.

I can't forget that.

* * *

"I fucking love the sun," Calla says as she rolls over on the towel next to Greer.

Greer, who in the last hour has made me realize that I have a lot less self-control than I ever imagined.

I'm a grown fucking man. But that woman makes me weak.

"Tell me about it. I have a to-do list a mile long at home, but when Simon mentioned the lake, I knew I'd be playing hooky on my responsibilities," Greer says, sitting up to apply more sunscreen to her shoulders.

I'm in a chair behind her. A fucking great smart spot, let me tell you.

I should have sat next to her. Or at least moved when she was lying on her stomach.

If I thought she looked good fully covered, my mind couldn't even put two sentences together when it saw her in a cheeky swimsuit.

I force my gaze out on the beach where Grey is tossing a football with Beck and Tobias. We invited the whole group, but not everyone can just make plans in five minutes.

Anyway, Grey tosses a perfect spiral.

I love that he has a passion. I worry he might be too obsessed with football because I feel like that's all he's done this summer outside of soccer and ninja warrior camp, but he could be into worse things, I suppose.

"I need to pee," my sister announces, jumping up and walking toward the marina that sits about a quarter mile away.

"Wait up," Beck shouts and jogs after her.

He swings an arm over her shoulders, and she looks at him just in time for a kiss.

I know, I know. It's my sister, I should be grossed out, right? But I'm not. I've never been happier for two people in my life.

I let out a sigh and return my gaze to the beach, only to come face-to-face with Greer's ass. Her perfectly round ass.

She spins to face me.

"Can you help me? I can't get my upper back."

If anyone were watching us right now, they would wonder why I'm staring at her and not saying anything.

She wants me to put my hands on her.

This is fine.

It's fine.

I stand, reaching for the sunscreen. With a healthy dollop squeezed into my hand, I do just as she asks. I start with both hands in the middle of her upper back and work them out in a circle.

"Get my shoulders again, please. Can't be too careful."

I take a breath, and her lavender shampoo hits me. God, she smells delicious. I rub over the top of her shoulder, my fingers bumping her straps.

Without a word, she reaches up to slip them off.

"That feels good," she says quietly.

Even though I know the sunscreen is rubbed in, I don't stop. I keep rubbing her back and shoulders. Somewhere along the way, I step closer. She tips her head to the side, and even though I'm supposed to be stopping, my hands rub her shoulders again, my fingers brushing toward her front more and more, rubbing her lower neck. She hums and adjusts her stance, bumping into me.

We both freeze.

Since my hands are still on her, I can feel the quick rise and fall of her chest the moment her breathing picks up. She turns slowly while I drop my hands and clear my throat.

"All set?"

Her eyes meet mine and she nods.

"Yes."

"Good."

I swallow, grinding my teeth as I keep my gaze locked on hers.

Kissing her would be wrong. It would complicate her role in helping me with Grey. It could affect her friendship with my sister. It would confuse us both.

But honestly, my need to see what she tastes like is screaming *fuck it.*

"Dad!"

Grey's voice cuts in, and I glance up just as Greer twists toward Grey.

Hell, I completely forgot we were on a beach in public with other people.

"Yeah?"

"You, me, and Aunt Calla against Tobias, Beck, and Greer."

"Oh great," Greer groans.

I nudge her arm. "You've been practicing in the yard with him, let's see what you've got."

An hour later, after Grey, Calla, and I have crushed the others, you'd think that my mind would have forgotten about the almost kiss with Greer, but it hasn't.

It may be the worst idea on the planet, but kissing Greer is officially on my to-do list.

Just one kiss can't hurt. Can it?

CHAPTER ELEVEN
GREER

Coming home to find Simon sitting on his porch is becoming routine for me. Had I moved in during the winter, I'm sure I wouldn't notice nearly as much. Nor would he need my services as a nanny slash housekeeper slash assistant or whatever you want to call me. The point is, I wake up, I go to work, and he's the first person I see when I come home. He's also the last person I see at night. And after this last weekend at the lake, every time I close my eyes to go to bed, all I see is him running shirtless on the beach or him standing in the doorway of his house.

The nights are getting hot, and Simon Stone is there, filling my dreams every single time.

I duck my head as I smile. It's not like he's watching for me and would see me smile at just the sight of him, but still. It's comforting to know that someone is waiting for me. Even if it's so I can hang out with their kid so they can do something else.

"Greer!" Grey comes blazing through the front door. His

dad raises his head, his gaze calm and cool as Grey races down the steps. "I have a huge favor to ask you."

"What's up?" I say and then turn my attention to Simon. "How's the writing going? Think about your favorite scene for today and tell me about it later."

As soon as the words are out of my mouth, it registers how flirtatious they were.

Simon smirks and closes his laptop.

"Today has been good. I forgot to mention a book signing I have later this afternoon. It's about two hours away in my hometown of Melody. I'm taking Grey with me since I'll be back late."

"Unless she wants to stay with me so I can go to camp this afternoon," Grey says, looking at me with hopeful eyes. "Please."

"No," Simon says in a tone that leaves no room for argument.

Grey clearly lets his father's answer go in one ear and out the other.

"But we didn't even ask her yet." He's also persistent.

"Grey, I'm sure she already has plans this evening. It could be close to midnight before I'm home."

I decide to step into their stare-down.

"I don't mind staying. It's not like I have a long drive ahead of me once you get home."

"I don't want to put you out."

I glare at Simon.

"You know you aren't. Grey is a great kid. Besides, we'll be asleep long before you get home. What trouble could we possibly cause in one afternoon?"

Simon stands and puts his hands on his hips. "You haven't hung out with my son long enough apparently."

"Is that a yes?" Grey asks. "Please, Dad. Please."

Simon's gaze catches mine, and I nod.

"I really don't mind."

He lets out a big groan, but he nods. "Fine. But you do as Greer says, and you're in bed by 9:30."

"Deal!" Grey says then high-fives me.

I laugh as he runs back into the house.

"Are you excited about your signing?" I ask.

"Signings are my favorite. I just didn't think of how much my career would impact Grey's life as he got older. When he was smaller, it was easier to just lug him around. He didn't argue. But it's clear, as you can see, that I need to make some changes over the next few years."

Simon packs his computer into his bag with jerky movements. Obviously, not being with Grey bothers him. If I weren't staying to take Grey to camp, I'd suggest that he and I surprise Simon.

I reach out to rub his arm.

"Hey, you'll figure it out. Some seasons of life are harder than others, but it doesn't mean you're doing anything wrong."

He pauses. As soon as his eyes fall on mine, I add, "You're doing a really good job, Simon. I'm not just saying that because you pay me or because of the vibe you're putting off either."

He shakes his head, but I see a faint smile.

"What kind of vibe am I giving off?"

"One that hints you're second-guessing this signing just so

you can stay with Grey. Go. He's going to be busy anyway. This is why you have me now."

Simon lifts his bag over his shoulder, pivoting to stand right in front of me. His expression is unreadable, but the way his eyes linger on my lips says enough.

It's probably best that he's leaving for the night. A little space would do us good. Being attracted to someone and not being able to do a damn thing about it is frustrating.

"Text me when you're home from camp, and then I'll text you later on to check in."

"You got it."

He opens the front door, stepping in to shout, "Grey, I'm leaving!"

Grey comes racing down the stairs, then he holds his hand up to high-five his dad.

I hear the slight groan Simon makes, but he hits his kid's hand and then hugs him.

"Dad, stop. I'll see you tomorrow."

Grey wiggles from the embrace and runs back up to his room.

Simon grabs his keys off the entry table, unlocking his truck.

"Oh, you're leaving right now, right now."

"Yeah, it starts in a few hours."

"You could have just called me. You didn't need to wait."

His mouth opens like he wants to say something, but instead he nods and steps around me.

"You two be good," he says.

"And you have fun. Try not to miss me too much," I tease.

He turns, walking backward, flipping his hat as he does so. "That's been pretty hard to do these days, Greer."

I have no words as he gets into his truck. I just bite my lip so he can't see the huge smile that wants to take over my lips.

I like flirty Simon.

Even when I shouldn't.

* * *

"He's just so handsome. I almost made Duke's father bring him today so I could go to the signing in Melody."

I reread the first sentence on my screen for the twentieth time as I hear another mom talk about Simon. They haven't outright said his name, but really, who else would they be talking about? Yes, I know a whole group of guys who write and could possibly be at this signing, but only one of them has a kid in this field right now.

"I know," another mom says before she lets her voice drop again. It's a little harder to hear, but I still make out her next words. "I miss when he would bring his son to camp. I was looking forward to getting to know him a bit more. As a single mom, it's hard to meet genuine guys these days. I was hoping I could get some one-on-one with him."

I laugh silently. I'd love to see any of them flirt with Simon. He may write romance novels, but I'm not so sure he's big on dishing out the type of chitchat she's clearly looking for. Then again, he did get a little flirty with me earlier, and he was good at it.

I cast my gaze at the gossiping moms. I don't like the idea of him flirting with any of them.

I swipe out of the book I was failing to read on my phone and pull up my planner. It's weird to look at it now that I'm not dating via apps. My personal schedule has a lot more free time. Hence why I was so open to watching Grey longer than normal today. In all honesty, I'm just a glorified driver of sorts. Grey doesn't need me for much of anything else but that. The rest of what I do is just a bonus, even if it's left me less time to find dates.

The coach blows his whistle, signaling the end of the day, and all the boys run off the field to get their things.

"I wasn't so sure we would see you today, Greer," one of the moms, who'd been talking about Simon, says as everyone stands to go meet their kids. "We assumed you'd be with Simon."

I should really get to know their names.

I give them a polite smile, and I'm just about to tell them why we didn't go when Grey pops up out of nowhere. "Dad wouldn't get anything done if Greer was there."

What does that mean?

Again, I'm about to inquire, but one of the moms beats me to it.

"Oh really? Why is that?"

I nod, cross my arms, and look at Grey. I, too, would like to know.

"Because they're dating, and he loves spending time with her."

My eyes nearly jump off my face as a collective gasp surrounds us.

"You're dating Simon Stone?"

"Why didn't you tell us?"

"That's sudden—how well do you know him?"

"I had no idea!"

Question after question rattles off while I keep my focus

on Grey, who's beaming. What am I supposed to say to that? Correct him, obviously.

"Simon and I are not—"

"We'll tone it down on our Simon chatter now that we know. I am so sorry—we had no idea."

They'll stop talking about him?

I could take that.

"You and Simon aren't what, Greer?"

"Huh?"

"You started to say something that you and Simon are not…"

"Telling a bunch of people yet. It's new," I blurt out. Grey is really grinning now.

Simon's going to kill me.

"Oh, well, our lips are sealed."

I'm sure.

"We should be going," I say quickly and put my hand on Grey's back to nudge him toward the car. I should get this kid out of here before he can come up with any other crazy stories.

However, the moment we get into my car, I twist to face him as he buckles himself into the backseat.

"Why did you say that?"

He shrugs one shoulder, pulling a water bottle from the cooler I've started keeping in the car for him.

"Because Billy kept saying that if my dad and his mom hit it off, we could be brothers, and I don't want to be brothers with Billy. All he talks about is video games. Dad needed a girlfriend fast."

I laugh at the disgust on his face.

"Do we tell him?" I ask Grey.

He shakes his head. "It's just the kids at camp. I think it can be our secret."

I'm not totally sure I agree, but he's right. No need to make this into something it's not. I can debate whether or not Simon needs to know later.

"All right, where to now?" I ask. "The night is young, Grey Stone."

"To get pizza!"

"What? Pizza?"

"Yep. We're already causing a ruckus, Greer. Let's be rebels for dinner and splurge for some ice cream too. I know where my dad keeps a hidden stash in the freezer."

This kid. He's much cheerier than his father, and I'll take it.

"That sounds like the perfect night."

I pull out of the parking lot and head for downtown Wind Valley to grab a pizza.

I know the summer isn't over yet, but moments like this, well, I'm really going to miss hanging out with Grey when they don't need me anymore.

Back to lonely ole boring Greer I will be.

The thought is sad, but then Grey starts to tell me all the jokes his teammates told him tonight, and you know what? Life is too short not to enjoy living in the moment.

Maybe that should be my motto for the rest of the summer. Stop dwelling on what has been or what will be and just be present.

The thought alone makes me feel lighter.

The possibilities are endless.

CHAPTER TWELVE
SIMON

It's been a long day, and sleep is calling my name as soon as I pull into the driveway.

Fuck. I almost missed the signing today. I should have left long before Greer showed up, but I wanted to see her. I hadn't planned for her to stay with Grey, but it worked out. Now, though, I wouldn't be upset if she were awake when I walked in the door.

I put my truck in park and let out a sigh.

I've been grateful for Greer since the day she started helping me out, but right now, I'm thinking I need to do something a little extra special for her. Knowing that Grey is in bed and my house is more than likely clean takes away more stress than I think she'll ever know.

Hell, the only stress I have now is controlling myself when I'm near her.

I grab my computer bag from the passenger seat, slinging it over my shoulder as I get out.

My stomach growls.

Signing days can be busy, and I forget to eat. Luckily for me, I've got a manager who remembers to bring snacks or steps out to get food for me while I'm working. The key, though, is to eat it when he tells me to.

Today, I'd skipped dinner to spend a little extra time with some readers who've decided to give writing a try. One of them was a man. I'm not saying you can't be a man and write romance—I'm evidence that it can happen—but it's not easy. We tend to get a little more judgment than others. Some readers have the opinion that a man can't give a heroine the characteristics or strength she deserves, but we can. I do. Anyway, he had a lot of questions about how to brand himself, and I didn't want to cut him short.

That said, I smell the remains of dinner in the air the moment I walk into the house from the garage.

I pause, closing my eyes and taking a deep breath.

A man could get used to this.

I move into the kitchen, set my bag on the kitchen table, and then open the fridge.

Right there on the middle shelf is a plate covered in Press 'n Seal with a sticky note.

Hope your hand hurts from signing lots of books. Don't heat this for longer than three minutes.
—Greer.

I take the plate, noticing the pizza box under it, and groan with joy as I see the fettuccine alfredo on the plate. She must have prepared this early in the day, but Grey clearly talked her into pizza. Typical.

My guess is this is the healthy version of pasta. Which,

having a health nut as neighbor and nanny means she" made enough trial-and-error dinner plates to find one that doesn" shout *this is health food!* the moment it hits your tongue.

It goes without saying that I inhale my late-night dinner in less than ten minutes.

I wash my plate, putting it in the dishwasher so as to not ruin the immaculately clean kitchen Greer left me with.

God. She really should let me pay her more. This isn't right.

If she won't take more money, I could dedicate the next book to her.

That's lame, but it's better than nothing.

I flip the light off and head upstairs. I didn't see Greer in the living room. I peek into Grey's room to see it, too, is cleaner than usual while he snores happily in bed.

I move down the hall to the spare room. I push the door open just slightly, and sure enough, she's curled up sound asleep under the sheets.

Her hair falls loose down the side of the bed, and one leg sticks out from the sheet she's covering herself with.

I take this moment to study her features. It's not common for me to observe her like this without the chance of her catching me gawking.

Which I do anytime she isn't looking. I can't help it. She does something to me that no other woman ever has. I loved Grey's mom, but Greer. I can't place it. She makes me feel something that both excites and terrifies me at the same time.

She takes a breath, her naked leg moving just barely and drawing my attention to the shorts she's wearing. From my angle, they barely cover her full cheek. The bottom sticks out just perfectly, enough for my mind to wander into areas it doesn't need to go.

Hell, she's asleep, and I'm thinking of how her ass would be the perfect handful. How her legs look like silk. Just touching them and running my hand between them would be enough to send me over the edge.

On another breath, I move my gaze from her body to her face. Perfect pink plump lips, long thick lashes, and a button nose.

She's fucking stunning.

Awake or asleep, I could watch her every moment of the day.

I move closer with the intention to wake her, because the longer I stand here, the more I want her and the more I shouldn't, but the moan that comes from her makes me freeze.

I swallow the lump in my throat.

Is she awake?

"Greer?" I say quietly.

She doesn't respond.

"Greer," I say just a touch louder.

Still nothing.

I let a moment pass, and she doesn't make another noise. Waking her is pointless. I'll just let her sleep here tonight. It would be wrong to wake her just so she can walk next door to another bed.

Will it be torture knowing she's in the bed in the room next to mine? Sure. But I can handle it.

I reach for the sheet and tug it gently so I can cover her completely.

But my movements aren't as soft as I wanted them to be.

"Simon," she says quietly as I'm leaning over her to fix the sheet.

I let my gaze drift to hers.

"Hi," I whisper.

"Hi," she whispers back.

Her sleepy gaze flashes from my eyes to my lips and back. I swallow.

We're alone. I'm aware of that. If I kiss her right now, there wouldn't be anyone to stop us. It wouldn't be just a stolen moment that lasts a second. I would want to take my time with her. I would need it. This woman has taken up too much time in my mind for me to not give her the attention she deserves.

She shifts, a subtle reminder that I'm still leaning over her, holding the sheet she's under.

I should move. It makes sense to move.

But I don't.

If anyone understands the debate that's taking over my brain right now, it's Greer. Her eyes glow up at me with silent permission to make the choice I want most.

I inch my face closer, my nose brushing against hers as I close my eyes.

"Stop me before I do something stupid," I whisper.

I feel her warm breath, minty from her toothpaste, as she takes focused breaths.

"I don't want to," she replies right before I crash my mouth to hers. I brace myself with a hand on each side of her head as she reaches too, threading her hands in my hair to hold on.

My tongue slips past her lips, deepening the kiss and eliciting a moan from Greer that could bring me to my knees.

I crawl over her, the sheet that started this whole event falling to the side as I rest one knee between hers. Her hips lift, brushing against me.

Hell, I knew she'd taste amazing. But this kiss—this kiss is seared to my memory now, and I know without a doubt that I will never be kissed the way she's kissing me. I will never kiss the way I'm kissing her. We fit. From the strokes of our tongues to the roll of our hips.

Our connection is kismet, and I don't give a fuck how cliché it sounds.

I tear my lips from hers and allow myself to gently kiss down her neck to her chest.

I should have known just one kiss wouldn't be enough for me.

"One last chance, Greer. Stop me before I do something stupid."

"No," she says, not missing a beat.

I continue to kiss down her body, the tiny tank top sliding up as my hands slip under it to cup her breasts.

"Shit, Greer. Your skin is so fucking soft, and it"—I pause to pull one of her nipples into my mouth— "tastes sweet too."

I move my attention to her other nipple and let it go with a pop.

"I knew it would."

"Then why didn't you try it sooner?" Her breathy question literally makes me growl.

"Because I knew once I had a taste, even just a small one, I wouldn't be able to stop."

"So don't."

I lift up to kiss her again, and as soon as her hand goes to my jeans, something inside me clicks.

Greer deserves more than a late-night fuck. Or, you know, wherever this is leading. I can't give her what she wants. I can't be who she wants.

As much as it pains me, I pull back and sit on the edge of the bed.

"What's wrong?" she asks, sitting up on her knees. "Was that too much?"

"No, fuck." I shake my head and rub my hands down my face. "It wasn't."

I stand quickly. She's too close, and I don't trust myself around her anymore.

"It's… I shouldn't have done that."

I'm too much of a chickenshit to look her in the eye, so I lift my head to catch her expression in the mirror that sits on the spare room dresser.

But the look she's giving me is void of any emotion.

"Okay," she says and crawls out of bed. She grabs a sweater that was folded on the corner of the dresser, and she walks by me. "I'll see you tomorrow."

That's it? She has nothing more to say to me? No fighting, yelling, or running away crying because she thinks she did something to repulse me? Nothing?

She just walks out of the room and down the stairs. I follow; a part of me thinks I just imagined everything that just happened.

Then again, the way my jeans rub against my hard dick says it was very real.

"You're just leaving?" I finally say. "You don't want to talk about it?"

She slips on her coat and then her shoes before spinning to

me. Her gaze locks on mine as she bites her lip, clearly debating her words.

"I'm pretty sure your mind is having the discussion for us."

She takes a step and cups my right cheek. My hands itch to grab her and continue what we started upstairs.

"Cut your inner debate short, okay? I get it. We were in the moment. It's fine. I'll see you tomorrow."

With that, she walks right out my front door.

Of course, I hover in the doorway, watching her every move until she's safely inside her house.

She turns her porch light off, so I do the same and head up to my room.

Greer is… fuck. Why does her reaction to what just happened make me want her even more?

I strip off my shirt and toss it into my laundry hamper that sits under my window.

A light from the house next door flicks on.

Greer stands in her window, looking right at me.

She brushes a finger across her chest at the seam of her top and watches me with a flirty smile. I step up, ready to see what more she'll do, but she reaches up and pulls the blinds shut.

Fuck me.

What did I just get myself into?

CHAPTER THIRTEEN
GREER

I slept like shit.

No, it wasn't because I fell asleep at Simon's only to be woken up to go to my own house. Disrupted sleep can be a huge pain in the ass. But I slept like shit because, even though I played it calm and cool, my body was screaming betrayal.

I can't remember the last time a man made me feel the way Simon did. And he only kissed me. Kissed my lips. My neck. My stomach. My chest.

Fuck.

I slap a hand on my forehead and roll over to look at the clock.

It's 4:36.

A perfect time to go for a morning run. Because, of course, my body has some pent-up energy it needs to get out.

I get up, change into some running clothes, and then stuff a backpack full of clean clothes. I'll go to the studio and get a workout in before my first client shows up at six this morning.

It's a full day, thank god. I have clients until I need to go grab Grey and take him to camp.

There'll be no time for me to think about Simon and the way his perfect soft lips felt against my body or about the way one touch made my body hum like it was going to let him do anything and everything he wanted.

"Ugh!" I growl as I step out the front door.

I pause in the yard to stretch, glancing up to his bedroom window.

His light is on, but I don't see him.

Good. I'm glad he can't sleep either.

I take off at a slow and steady pace, deciding to take the long route to work today.

Look, I get it, okay. Simon and I are clearly attracted to each other and have been dancing around it for weeks now. Last night was bound to happen. The pull we have to each other was too strong to not bring us together. I also get that we want different things. I'm very open about what I want in life. Simon isn't. So I wouldn't be surprised if he never plans to settle down again. So yeah, his stopping us was probably for the best. But hell, it would have been so good.

I round the first corner and have two options: big hill or no hill.

I pick the big hill.

Because I like to punish myself, clearly.

At least it'll give my brain something else to think about.

* * *

I've worked out three times today, and it's only eleven.

Yep. It's safe to say that I'm unsuccessfully avoiding thoughts of Simon.

It didn't help that my first client, Mr. Chapman, brought his wife, and I swear they're in honeymoon phase number two. The one where their youngest just moved out, and it's just the two of them all over again.

So they were flirty and cute as hell.

It made me think of Simon and how the only woman I've ever seen him flirt with is me.

Then Kate Stamper came in, and the first thing she did was crack a joke about how her left arm was hurting from lugging around her brand-new engagement ring. To which she recited all the adorable proposal details to me. It made me think about how many proposal scenes Simon has ever written.

After Kate came, Suanne showed up, and guess what? After twelve years of dating apps, she finally met a man who she's successfully gone on six dates with. She thinks I should reactivate my accounts and keep going, but all I could think about was how useless that would be. I'm crushing on the single dad next door, and there's nothing I can do about it.

Needless to say, when Natalie Miller comes in for her session, a friend I trust, I blurt out the first thing my mind thinks of while we're stretching.

"Simon kissed me," I say quickly and then fall back into child pose. "And my neck and lower, and I don't know how many details you want, but it happened."

"What?" she asks, fighting a smile. "When?"

"Last night." I come up to a sitting position and scrunch my nose. "He had a signing in Melody, so I stayed late with Grey. I was asleep in the spare room by the time he got home.

I'd planned to just sleep there all night. I didn't think he would wake me up."

"And he did so he could kiss you." She claps and squeals.

"Not exactly." I reach for my toes. "I think he was trying to cover me, but I woke up. It was like my body knew he was near, and we couldn't waste that time by sleeping."

"Cute!"

"Not cute," I deadpan. "This is Simon. Calla's brother. Grumpy Simon who, until I was working for him, barely put two sentences together anytime I spoke to him."

Natalie shimmies her shoulders. "And now he's replaced those words with kisses."

I shove her shoulder and move into another pose. "Stop. No. It was—"

"Don't tell me he's a bad kisser."

"Not even close." I smile. "But he did cut it off and say he shouldn't have done that."

Natalie groans.

"Classic. Why do guys do that?"

I shake my head. "No clue."

"So then what happened?"

I shrug. "I went home."

"That's it?"

I nod.

"Damn. So what now?"

"I don't know. I told him we didn't need to talk about it, but all I can think about is how I haven't found time for dating since I started watching Grey and now this happens."

Natalie holds up her hand. "Question," she says, and then holds up one finger. "First, why can't you date Simon?"

"Because for as long as I've known him, he hasn't dated

anyone. If he wanted to date me, I think he'd have asked by now."

"Okay, that's fair. Second"—she holds up another finger — "if you don't have time to date right now, why not have fun? If you and Simon don't want to date but are clearly into each other, technically kissing isn't dating, soooo… what's the big deal?"

I stare at her. Huh. That's true.

"Either way, he stopped it. I don't know why, and I'm not going to ask. I actually want to date someone. Not just have fun."

"But do you like him?"

She barely gives me time to answer before she grins.

"You totally do."

"I do."

"So why don't you not date him for a while?" She winks. "At least until you meet someone worth dating for real."

It's not the worst idea, but given his choices last night, I don't think he wants that.

I sigh and shake my head. "I think I'm doomed for a summer of sexual tension."

"Bummer."

Total bummer for sure, because as much as I'll tell myself not to, I won't be able to be around Simon ever again without thinking of the way his body felt against mine.

Summer of sexual tension? More like summer of pure torture.

CHAPTER FOURTEEN
SIMON

"I think I've got a problem." I lower my computer screen. Any time one of us mentions having a problem with our current work in progress, our group as a whole is ready to dive in to fix it as quickly as possible. So they all stop what they're doing to look up, and I feel guilty that it has nothing to do with writing.

"Chapter development?"

"Plot?"

"What act are you on?"

I scrub my hand over my face and groan. "It's not with writing. It's with Greer."

I could have beat around the bush, but I need advice and want to get this conversation over as quickly as possible. I'm not one to sit around and talk about my feelings. Plus, I've been the guy on the other end of this conversation, and I know how carried away we can get with personal topics. The fact we all write romance only adds fuel to the discussion.

"What about her?" Beck asks.

"Did she do something wrong?" Tobias asks. "Is Grey okay?"

I nod. "Everything is good. She's great with Grey. Too great, maybe. I don't know. Fuck." I sit up straighter. "I kissed her last night while she was lying in the spare room bed."

As expected, silence follows from everyone except…

"I knew it!" Beck cheers. "Yes. Oh, Calla is going to be so excited. She called this. I told her she was nuts, but she knew. God, she's right more times than I like to admit."

He's already reaching for his phone.

"Whoa, whoa, calm down. I don't know if it means anything."

Hero laughs. "Okay, try that again. You kissed her, Simon. You know it means something, otherwise you wouldn't have done it. The real question is, what do you want it to mean?"

I let out a breath. "I… I don't know. I—" They are all going to hate this next part. "I stopped it before we could get carried away."

"Typical," Tobias says, and even though others in the group have their opinion, I know his response has a different meaning.

"You know she wants to settle down, right? Willa told me," Zane adds as his fingers find their way back to his keyboard. "Even if you wanted it to mean something, from your track record, it wouldn't mean what she'd want it to mean."

Beck guffaws. "But if they're meant to be together, what it means to each of them will change within time, and it could be wonderful."

Tobias lets out a deep chuckle. "One day he's all *oooh she gets on my nerves* and the next he's married in Vegas on a whim, a believer of fate, and the biggest romantic of the group."

Beck punches Simon's arm. "I had my chance, and I wasn't about to lose it."

"Anyway," I say, bringing the topic back to me because I'd rather keep talking about this than my sister's love life, "the problem is, she wasn't even mad that I stopped it. She just said *okay* and went home. Then she told me not to over-think it."

"Which you are clearly doing." Zane chuckles.

Graham closes his laptop with a thud. "If you like her, just ask her out. If you don't want to date her, forget about it. Address it if she brings it up. Otherwise, do as she said and don't overthink it."

I nod. "Seems too easy."

"Take it from me. Don't avoid it. Just talk to her."

"Make sure you know what you want first," Zane says. "Don't make it weird, since she works for you."

"Huh," Graham says. "I forgot about that part."

"Figure it out quickly because she and Grey are about to walk through the door," Hero says. All six of us shift.

Greer pauses just inside the door.

"Is everything okay?" she asks cautiously.

"Everything is fine," I answer before one of these guys says something stupid.

Grey struts in, takes a seat next to Beck, and asks him what he's working on. My attention quickly goes to the brunette beauty slowly walking toward me with a shy smile on her lips. There was nothing shy about them last night, and I'm about two seconds from reminding her of this small fact.

"Oh good," she says. "Grey and I were just walking back

to the house from his ninja warrior camp and thought we would drop off a smoothie for you. It has protein and other goodies to help with energy. I thought you might need some after last night."

Someone near me snorts, but I refuse to look to see who it is.

Are these my friends or Grey's friends?

"That is so sweet of you, Greer," Graham says. "Thinking of Simon."

I clear my throat and glare over my shoulder at my friend.

"Is it chocolate peanut butter?" I ask, returning my attention to Greer.

She nods.

"Perfect." I grab the drink and take a sip.

"Dad, can I have a couple friends sleep over after my birthday party next weekend?"

"That sounds fine to me."

"Your birthday is next week?" Greer asks. "I had no idea."

She ruffles Grey's hair, and he swats her hand away, laughing.

"Is there anything I can help with?" she asks me.

"Actually, yes. He wanted to invite all his football camp friends, so I sent a message through this app we all use. Some of the parents commented that they'd be staying, so I think I need to double the order I originally planned and—" Greer's eyes widen. "Why are you looking at me like that?"

"Ummm, you said football camp parents are going to come?"

"Yes."

"Okay, well, funny story about that. Impeccable timing too." She looks over my shoulder and I follow her gaze to see everyone invested in her story. I could scold them, but I just shake my head.

"Can we talk in private?" she asks a little quieter.

I nod, knowing the guys will eavesdrop if we stay here. I move her to the back room where our office is. I know it seems weird that we opened a working space with an office in the back, but some days, usually at the beginning of the week, this place is packed shoulder to shoulder. I need to know I can come here and have a place to write. So we created the office. Funny enough, I think the whole group is glad we have it.

We step inside. "Should I close the door?"

"No. Sure. Maybe." She fidgets with her purse.

I choose to close the door.

I've been alone with a woman many times in my life, but right now, all my senses are on overdrive thinking about how I'm alone with Greer. Again. My heart beat picks up, and my breathing feels uneven.

Hell, I don't know how to control myself when I'm around her. I want her. That much is clear.

I just can't have her. My conversation with the guys is evidence enough. She wants to meet someone and get married. I don't want to date anyone period. I may as well have a red flag attached to my forehead for her.

But my body remembers everything about last night. Despite knowing why this shouldn't happen, I want it to.

I move toward her.

"The thing is," she says, looking me right in the eyes, "the football camp moms might all think that you and I are dating."

I stop.

"What?"

"I know. I *know*." She begins to pace. "It all happened so fast."

I almost laugh—oh, the irony! —but Greer looks so distraught, I pull it together.

"Why do they think we're dating, Greer?"

Honestly, I'm not even mad that someone would think that, but I am intrigued to know how this came about and how long we've been together, considering Grey's last football camp afternoon, before I kissed her, was just yesterday. What exactly has she been up to?

"Grey told them that we were, and I didn't deny it."

I can't help it. I laugh. That kid of mine is something else. I love him.

"It's not funny, Simon. I only went along with it because all they do is talk about you, and once they heard we were dating, they apologized and said they'd stop."

I rub my chin. "Oh, so you were jealous?"

"What? Of them talking about you? No. It's just annoying to listen to it for close to six hours a week."

"Last night hints that you might have been jealous." I smirk.

She punches my shoulder.

"Stop it. Don't tease about that."

"No?" I say and step toward her. She bumps into the desk, and I know I shouldn't kiss her again, but fuck, I want Greer more than I've wanted anything in a long, long time. Staying away from her is like asking a kid to hold a bag of candy and not eat it.

"Simon, are you about to do something stupid?"

Her words make me pause. Yes, I was. It would have been

worth it. But continuing to tease, as Greer puts it, isn't something I want to do to her.

"Well, okay then." I back up.

"Okay then, what?" she asks and holds her hands up. "What do we tell them at the party? Oh, wait, I'll just not go. I'll hide in my house, and you tell them I'm working."

Again, she just moves on from whatever could have happened between us so easily. Is it possible I'm imagining the amount of attraction we have toward one another?

"You can't miss Grey's party, Greer."

"Ugh. I know it."

She flops down into the chair and swivels right to left. Did she think I would be upset? Faking a relationship wasn't exactly on my plans for this summer, but it's one afternoon, and right now, I'd do anything to help Greer after all she's done for me.

"So what will we do?" she asks.

I sit across from her; grateful Tobias convinced me to get more than just a single desk chair in this room.

"We just tell them that we're dating. It's one party. It's going to be fine."

She stares past me at the door.

"One party. Yeah. I can do that."

"Good. And it'll probably work better if we keep this between us. The fewer people who know, the better chances we have to pull this off."

"I agree."

She relaxes back into the chair, turning to give me a smile.

"I better go get Grey and get out of your hair so you can get some work done."

She stands quickly, giving me a small wave as she walks out the door.

But I don't move right away—her words hit me.

I know that's what I hired her for, so I could have time to get work done. But right now, the last thing I want is for her to go. I'm growing used to having Greer around, and the idea of her not being there someday when I get home doesn't sit well with me.

When I finally decide to rejoin the guys in the main room, Greer and Grey are still standing around talking to everyone.

I smile but quickly rub my nose to hide it before anyone notices. These guys are all about the small details.

I step up behind Grey, my hands on his shoulders as I ask, "Where are you two off to?"

"Uncle Beck said I could stay with him and Calla tonight. Can I?"

I glance at Beck, who is grinning.

"I thought it might be nice to have a night off. Besides, it's been weeks since Calla and I had Grey over to stay up all night watching horror movies and eating junk food."

I glare at my friend and then look at Grey's hopeful face.

"Please, Dad, please."

"Fine. But you need to do whatever Greer asks this afternoon, got it?"

"Yes!" He turns to me with his hand up for a high five.

"Come on, Greer!" He races for the door. "We have things to do."

She laughs and follows him, walking backward as she waves goodbye.

As soon as they're out the door, I take my spot back in

front of my computer, praying I can get back into the head-space to keep writing. Greer is starting to take more of my thoughts than the words I need to put on the screen.

I get maybe a few hundred words in when it registers how quiet the room is.

I look up. Everyone is looking at me.

"What?" They all make some sort of disapproving noise. Apparently, my one-word question was not what they wanted to hear.

"You're kidding, right?" Beck asks.

"About what?"

"Greer," Zane says. "You two are totally into each other."

I shrug, but then Greer and I are fake dating for the party next weekend, and maybe saying that they're wrong won't help us. Then again, these are my friends. I can tell them everything, right?

When no one else comments, I notice I'm still the center of attention.

Maybe I'll just keep the fake dating plan to myself for now.

Instead, I smile, thinking of how Greer must have felt in that moment with the football moms.

"We'll see," is all I say.

"I knew it," Beck says, finally turning his focus back to his computer.

The others just chuckle and get back to work.

Ten minutes later, I've found my groove, but Beck slaps the table.

"It just occurred to me that you'll be alone tonight."

I laugh.

"Yep."

"You should invite Greer over."

And that's the only thing my brain can focus on for the rest of the afternoon.

CHAPTER FIFTEEN
GREER

I hate to let good food go to waste.

I slip into Simon's house, knowing he'll be here any minute, and head straight for the kitchen. I'd made a buffalo chicken casserole that just needed to be put in the oven for half an hour. I turn the oven on and take the prepared dish out of the fridge. Just as I'm pulling back the Press 'n Seal, the door to the garage opens and Simon steps inside. His house isn't small by any means, but right now, his kitchen feels smaller than a cubical.

"Hi," I say quickly. "I was hoping to be gone before you got here."

Just a little wishful thinking on my part that the oven would heat up faster than it's ever warmed up ever before. I should have just taken the casserole to my house, but Simon pays me to cook, too, so that wouldn't really work out.

Maybe I should have just left him a sticky note with instructions.

"Hi," he says, moving into my space and setting his bag

down on the counter. One thing I've noticed is that his computer bag goes wherever he goes. I appreciate his dedication to his career. I should definitely add that to my list of qualities in a man.

I point to the dish in front of me. "I prepped this earlier before I knew Grey was going with Calla and Beck for the night. I didn't want it to go to waste."

"So you were going to just put it in my oven and leave?"

I nod.

"What if I didn't come home tonight?"

I pause. If he didn't come home, where would he go? I never knew not coming home was an option for him.

"I would have set a timer on my phone. Like I said, I didn't want it to go to waste. Plus, this is one of my favorite dishes. Trust me when I say, someone was going to be eating this tonight."

He chuckles.

"A few weeks working for me, and you've just made yourself right at home in my kitchen."

Among other places, but for obvious reasons, I don't say that out loud.

However, the look he's giving me says he knows exactly what I'm thinking.

I shrug, as if him standing right in front of me and reading my mind doesn't faze me and give him a sweet smile. "You've got a cute kid. He makes me feel extremely welcome here."

The grin on Simon's face slowly fades. "I'm sorry about that. Grey shouldn't be the only one making you feel that way. I enjoy having you around, Greer. I like that you move around this house as if it were your own."

He stops speaking, but his mouth remains open, as if he wants to say more.

He chooses not to. The list of things he and I need to discuss is growing quickly.

I almost tell him that the hustle and bustle of his and Grey's busy life feels much more my style, but I don't say a word either. The reality is, I'm just here to help. This won't be forever. If I mix feelings about last night and whatever we want to call the job I'm actually here for, it'll be harder for me at the end of the summer when they don't need me anymore. I don't want this to be weird between us. Perhaps that's the reason we don't talk about all the things we should.

"Well, anyway," I say, grabbing my purse off the table and backing toward the hallway to leave out the front, "once the oven goes off, just put the dish in for thirty minutes. Let it cool for another five before you eat it. There's a cucumber and tomato salad ready in the fridge for your side."

I give him a small wave, and just as I'm spinning on my toe, he says, "Why don't you stay and eat with me?"

Two things happen at that moment. First, my heart rate increases, and second, confusion completely takes over my expression. Did Simon Stone willingly just invite me to hang out with him? Not because I'm friends with his sister or because his son begged him to ask me, but because he wants me to?

"Oh, I—"

"You did mention this was your favorite dish, and there's no way I can eat all this alone."

The idea is tempting, but is it smart? Is eating dinner with a man who hired me for the summer to help with his son and with whom I made out with in his spare room less than twenty-four hours ago really a good idea?

No, it's a bad idea.

Very bad.

"I don't want to impose on your night alone. I'm sure they're rare for you, and you have things you'd rather be doing."

He gives one single slow nod. "What I'd like to do is eat some food, have a beer or two on my back patio, and do both of those things with good company. So, will you stay?"

And beer! This is just a red flag city. It's a bad, bad idea.

"I'd love to."

* * *

"My stomach hurts, but in a good way," Simon says and stands to stretch. "I ate way too much. It was worth it."

I laugh and sip my beer. It's my second. I call it my after-dinner beer, which means I should stay for only this one and then be on my way.

Go home.

Not hang around any temptation, as my body clearly has decided to relax in his presence.

Turns out, grumpy ole Simon Stone has a sense of humor, and you can bet it's not helping my mental state right now.

I like funny. I want funny. I'll add it to the list.

Simon raises his hands above his head, and his shirt rises just enough for me to see his bare stomach.

Holy mother of god. He has the lines. The lines! The ones that are like a flashing neon sign to look lower and cause my mind to short-circuit on real words.

I look away before he catches me, and, you guessed it, I take another sip.

At this rate, I should be home in about five minutes. Especially since my mind is now filled with what I just saw. The more time I spend with Simon, the more my body acts as if it has no control.

"This might go against your personal rules, but I do have dessert." He flashes me a smile and steps for the sliding door.

"If it's the chocolate swirl ice cream you hide under the edamame in the freezer, Grey and I are fully aware."

He freezes and looks at me with horror. I laugh.

"What? You have a ten-year-old son, Simon. If you think he hasn't searched every inch of that kitchen for junk food, you're in for a surprise."

"He's never said a word to me about it. Wait, are you saying it's gone?"

I shake my head. "No. We just know about it and replace it when we eat it."

He grins. "How often do you eat ice cream?"

"Oh, Simon," I say sweetly. "I break the rules more than you think."

And then I wink, pretending I didn't just hear the amount of flirting laced in my voice in the last ten seconds. He's a romance writer. He writes sex. Will his mind go there immediately?

Suddenly, he's towering over me, and the heated look in his eyes says yes, yes, his mind did go there.

"Anyway, there's plenty left for you."

I wave him away with my beer bottle and take another drink.

He moves quickly, and I hear the freezer door slam shut

and then the silverware drawer jerking open as if someone were furious at it for doing something wrong.

Then he stomps back outside, thrusting a spoon in my face.

I almost laugh because, although I'm a little embarrassed about my remark, I didn't expect him to have this reaction. Or maybe I did and I'm just wishing that I didn't wish for it.

It's almost like he's… I don't know. Maybe he's just as frustrated with what's happening between us as I am.

We both know it can't lead anywhere. It's an unspoken agreement, so there's no point in acting on the attraction we have.

Not again, anyway.

At the same time, we can't just shut it off.

He pulls the top off the ice cream pint and holds the pint between us, taking a large scoop for himself. He licks the ice cream instead of just sticking the whole spoon in his mouth; his tongue flattens to touch both sides of the spoon so that he doesn't miss anything.

He stops, and that's when I glance up to see that he's caught me watching him.

I quickly grab a spoon full for myself. It's not a dainty one either.

Unlike Simon, I stick the whole spoon into my mouth.

He chokes.

"Fuck."

He hits his chest with a closed fist, and I just laugh.

"Look, I hate confrontation, but this whole eye contact and pretending we aren't attracted to each other thing we're doing is mentally exhausting."

So much for an unspoken agreement. Clearly, I need one out loud.

As if he didn't hear anything I just said, Simon keeps his eyes on me.

"Do I need to take another bite, or do you want to talk?"

He sighs.

"I don't know what to say."

I sit up straighter and set my spoon down. He does the same.

"Just say the first thing that comes to mind," I tell him.

"I can't."

"Simon, we need to find a way to move past this. I can't keep showing up here thinking of what you look like naked and never knowing."

The beer he just sipped sprays from his mouth. He stands and starts to brush the beer spots off his shirt.

"Jesus, Greer."

"What? I'm tired of beating around the bush and"—I hold up my beer and stand directly in front of him— "two beers later clearly means I'm not afraid to speak my mind. So humor me, please, let's talk about this."

"You want to talk about it, fine. I can't even wake up without thinking about you. I can't write a single word on my front porch without hoping to catch a glance of you. I count down the minutes until you show up at my house each day, and you're not even here for me."

Oh, wow.

WOW.

My first thought is to climb on him and kiss him, but I try my best to rein in my reaction.

"Oh, that's sweet."

"And that," he says, stepping in front of me. "Nothing I say fazes you. Ever. You just understand. Hell, I don't even understand what I just said."

"It's not that I understand what you're saying, Simon. It's that I understand you. Something is stopping you from taking what you want. I don't know what it is, but I know enough to give you space to find out."

The words are barely out of my mouth when he presses his lips to mine, cupping my face with his hands. I melt into him, tossing my empty drink on the chair behind me so that I could grip his shirt.

He backs us up until he hits his chair. He sits, pulling me on top of him. Our lips never break from devouring each other. As soon as my hips start to move, guided by the rise of his own, he groans. It fuels me to move faster. I smooth my hands down his shirt, sneaking them under it to feel the ripples of his abs. He takes this as a sign to help me out of my shirt, but as he starts to lift the hem, he stops.

"Greer, wait." He lets out a big breath, closes his eyes, drops his head back. "I can't—"

I don't even wait for him to finish this time.

Like I told him, I'm a very understanding person, but a girl can only be turned down so many times before she cracks. And right now, it's my turn. The beer might have helped escalate my emotional state.

I crawl off him and race into the house, grabbing my things as I head for the front door. I'm just off the porch when I hear him behind me.

"Greer, wait, please."

"No."

"Please. Let's talk for a moment."

"We don't need to. Not anymore."

"Yes, we do."

"We really don't, Simon." I try to go back to what I was doing.

I let myself get carried away. I let myself think about things I shouldn't have, and it's nobody's fault but my own.

"You're crying, Greer. Let me explain."

"It's really fine. I'm fine."

"I know you're lying. Look, I'm sorry."

"The words every girl wants to hear after a man kisses her. *Again.*" I take a breath, wipe under my eyes, and then force a smile as I look at him. "See—all better. I'm going to go if you don't need me for anything else."

"Greer." Simon is hot on my heels as I cross the grass between our houses. "Believe me when I say those are the last words I want to say, but we… this… I can't give you what you want."

"Then why are you following me? Why not just let me go home?"

He sighs.

"I…"

His lips part like he's going to say something, but then he looks back to his house for a split second before his eyes find mine again. A moment passes, and he doesn't say another word. I toss my hands up and let out a breathy laugh.

"Wow," is all I say before I walk away.

"I don't know what I'm doing." He stalks toward me. "But seeing you cry is something I never want to see again."

"Oh, I'm sorry, did I make you sad?"

"Jesus, Greer. You and that smart-ass mouth." He shakes his head. "Sad, no. Mad? Hell fucking yeah. I'm not this guy.

The one who cares this much, but you, you make me…" He pauses, taking over the pacing I was doing moments ago. His fingers tug at his hair, leaving it with pieces sticking up all over. "I've never wanted to play the hero for someone, not till you came along, and I have no idea how to feel about that."

His breathing is heavy as he backs up to his house. I don't think he's expecting a response. I think... I don't know what to think.

"The last thing I want to do is hurt you, Greer. I promise. But for some crazy reason, I can't seem to stay away from you. I know I should, but I can't."

I bite my bottom lip, but I still don't say anything. What would I say? He's standing here telling me that he wants me but won't let himself have me. How do I process that?

I want to be mad, but I'm not.

My heart actually hurts thinking of what it must be like to be in his head right now.

He tugs at his hair and rubs his neck.

How can I be mad when he's so honest?

He steps toward me and stops. "I don't want to end this night in a fight. Not with you, but if I stand here any longer not touching you, I'm afraid I'll hurt you even more."

I nod.

"So, I'm going to go inside now, all right?"

I nod again.

But I don't move, and he chuckles. "Greer, you know I can't go inside my house until you're safely inside yours."

Like before, I nod. But I do head inside.

I lean against my door, my purse dropping to the floor next to me.

I should have said more.

A lot more.

He made this choice on his own, this choice that something between us can't happen.

It takes two people, and I should get a say, right?

I tap my chin.

Simon and I do want different things. I get that. But maybe I'm thinking about this all wrong. Maybe Natalie was right. Maybe I need something not serious. Something carefree. Something to relieve the stress of my goal taking longer than I want.

Simon and I could still have fun, right?

CHAPTER SIXTEEN
SIMON

Sleeping is nonexistent tonight.

I glance at the clock. Shit. It's only nine. This is going to be a long night.

I head up the stairs, peeking into Grey's room as I head down the hallway to mine. I know he isn't here, but it's a habit I don't think I'll kick anytime soon.

I pull his comforter up, straighten a few of the football books on his shelf, and then I turn out the light.

Will it be a mindless episode of *The Office* tonight, or should I grab my computer and get ahead on a few things?

My hand is on my bedroom light switch when a movement beyond my window catches my eye. Specifically, through Greer's window.

I don't think she can see me, but she's staring at my house as if she's looking for me. Her hand is playing with the collar of her shirt as she bites her bottom lip.

Oh hell.

It's on her mind too. All the things we could be doing if I hadn't broken the kiss and if she hadn't run off.

It's my fault. I know it is, but fuck, Greer is good. Too good. I'd ruin the friendship we've built and lose her. I can't afford that, and I sure as hell don't want to be the reason she ever cries again. A part of me thinks I should have just said fuck it and dealt with the consequences later. You know, that mindset of having her just once to get her out of my system. But I'm not an idiot. We all know how that works. Me? I chose the *I'm so sorry route* each time we kissed.

Maybe I *am* an idiot.

I look back to the window, never taking my eyes off her as she stands there.

What's she waiting for?

She reaches for something on her nightstand.

Her phone.

She types something quickly and then looks up.

My phone buzzes.

I pull it from my pocket, and the screen lights up my room.

Shit.

Another text comes through immediately.

I let out a sigh.

Hey.

I knew you were there.

I start to type out *yep* but think better of it. This is Greer. I'm tired of pretending like she doesn't faze me. She does. She unnerves me so badly that I can't stand it, but hell, I'll suffer if it means more time with her. And if she gives me one more chance, I'm not going to stop it.

I'm sorry. I shouldn't have pulled away.

Her text is instant.

I shouldn't have run. I should have just talked to you. So I'm sorry too.

She looks up, and I see the faintest smile.

Can I come over?

No.

But you can watch.

Oh hell. Four words. Four simple words was all it took for my mind to process a hundred scenarios of what *but you can watch* would mean, sending a signal to my groin to wake up.

I take a deep breath, my thumb hovering over the keypad, when another text comes in.

Move so I can see you.

I take a deep breath and do as she says. Her wide smile makes my heart feel as if she were squeezing it.

No one's smile has ever done that to me.

Before I can think too much about how it makes me feel, she slowly inches her fingers to the inside of her thighs, then pulls her T-shirt up higher, as if she's going to pull it over her head. When all I see are the little spandex shorts she has on underneath, she loops her fingers in the sides and pulls them down her legs. Her oversized T-shirt hides enough that I can't see her but sits high enough that just the slightest movement would give me a peek.

My cock strains against my jeans.

I wait with bated breath for her to make the next move, but she grins and holds up her phone.

I glance down at the text I didn't know she sent.

Jesus, is that what she does to me? She pulls me out of reality and into a world where nothing exists but her. It's terrifying. I know I can't have her forever, but I want more.

> Your turn. This is how it works. I make a
> move. You make a move.

I read her text three times, nodding the entire time, before tossing it to my bed. I strip my T-shirt off as if my life depended on it.

I keep my eyes trained on Greer to gauge her reaction. She inhales a big breath and bites her bottom lip again.

I raise my brow and grin. I'm convinced that she can read my mind.

Your turn.

Her cheeks flush a little as she, too, pulls her shirt over her head. She's got on another one of those strappy black lace bras. The sight brings me back to the moment I first saw it that day downstairs. I'll tell you what, my imagination didn't do her justice. She looks sexier than I ever dreamed.

Next, I slowly take my belt off, pulling it in one swift motion, the way the heroes do in all my books, and drop my jeans. I see that Greer has moved closer to her window; the moonlight illuminating her even more than before.

I do the same, and when she turns to show me that she's wearing a thong and gives me a full display of her perfect perky globes of an ass, I can't help it, I reach right into the front of my boxers and grip myself.

"Fuck," I say loudly on a groan.

My eyes start to close, imagining that it's Greer who's got a hold of me and that she's the one slowly moving her hand up and down.

As much as I want to keep this image of her, I want to see the real her more. So I open my eyes and catch her doing the same thing I am. Her hand is in the front of her panties and her head is tilted back; her lips parted, displaying the perfect circle.

Fuck this.

With my free hand, I grab my phone and call her.

The noise startles her, but she picks up by the third ring.

"Simon," she answers in a breathy tone.

"Greer," I all but growl, "if you think you can make me watch and not touch you, fine, but I'll be damned if I don't get to hear the noises you make when you think of me as you come."

"Okay" is all she says.

"Now, lay on your bed. On the corner where I can still see you."

She does it.

Fuck all if I'm going to let her continue to stand in her window where anyone but me could see her.

"Good girl. Now, do everything I tell you to do."

"Simon, should we be doing this?"

"Baby, there is nothing more I want to be doing than watching you right now."

"I know, but earlier—"

"Don't think, Greer, just listen to me and let me make you feel good."

She doesn't reply right away, but I hear her breathing pick up right before she finally says, "What do you want me to do?"

I swear to god I could come in my hand just hearing her asking me for orders.

I had no idea I could be this controlling in bed, but hell, with Greer, there isn't another way I'd want it.

"Lift your hips and slide your panties all the way off. Let me see you."

She doesn't even think twice. She just does as she's told. I grow harder at her obedience.

"Now what?"

"Now slide your fingers between your legs, slowly. Pretend it's me."

Her hand moves.

"Yes, god, you're so soft. I knew your skin would be like silk."

Her hand dips between her legs.

"Now, slide a finger inside your pretty pussy."

My hand moves faster.

"Yes," she breathes on the phone.

"Yeah, baby. Do you like that?"

"I do."

"Add another finger."

She moans.

"Fuck, Greer. I love listening to you. That's right, baby.

Give yourself more pressure. Imagine my cock pumping in and out of you."

I'm a fucking fool for stopping her earlier. The next time I get her in my arms, I'm not letting her go. Will it end badly? Maybe. But I'll hate myself if I never give it a chance.

"Are you thinking of me?" she whispers.

"Baby, I couldn't think of anything else even if I tried."

"Do you like what you see?"

"Oh yeah."

"Good, because I need you to help me finish. Tell me what you would do to me if you were here."

I wish like hell I was.

"I'd move my hand faster, and when your back bows—yes, like it is now—I'd pull my fingers out and replace them with my tongue. I'd suck on you, flicking my tongue until my name was falling from your lips."

"Simon," she says. "Simon, yes."

She doesn't have to tell me she's coming; I can see it by the steady movement of her hips and the way her free hand runs through her hair.

A sensation rips through me, and I hold my breath until every last bit of me is spent in my hand.

"Fuck, Greer," I growl. I came harder than I've come in my entire life. If this is what it's like when she isn't even touching me, I'm going to be totally screwed when she does.

I pull my hand from my boxes, stepping into my bathroom to wash my hand quickly so that I don't miss another moment of Greer on her bed.

When I step back, she's on her side, watching me with the phone against her ear.

Even with the distance between us, her eyes stare right

into my soul. That look, the one of pure happiness, is the only look I want to see in her eyes from this moment on.

The thing is, I don't deserve a woman like Greer.

And she sure as hell deserves more than I can give her.

I'm just too selfish to give her up now.

CHAPTER SEVENTEEN
GREER

It's been a whole week since Simon and I had phone sex.

There's no way to sugarcoat it, and there's no way we can avoid talking about it either. Not for much longer anyway.

Luckily for me, I don't work for him today. I still have to go over there later for Grey's party, but if there's one thing Simon and I are good at, it's avoiding any serious conversation and acting like everything is normal. I bet we avoid this one for a whole month.

My phone buzzes in my purse, so I pull it out, seeing a scheduling text from a client. I grab my planner next to switch their appointment.

Work and Grey are the two reasons Simon and I haven't talked about the other night. We've both been so busy, and it's nice, but we can't avoid it forever. I would text him, but it's definitely a conversation that should happen face-to-face. At the same time, if I look him in the eyes when we talk about what we did or any part of his body I saw him stroke or touch that night, I'm not so sure I can keep the lust out of my eyes.

And if he kisses me one more time and then apologizes, I very well might be the next feature of women who snap. Okay, okay, so that's a bit extreme. But I'd probably have to quit, and that would be devastating.

I'm attracted to Simon. There's no denying it. And as much as I would love to say that I have self-control, if he touched me again, despite the war in my brain, I would give in. It's been so long since a man has made me feel the way he did, and that was only over the phone. It was my own hands. I can't imagine the pleasure that would come from him actually touching me.

Hell, from him speaking to me the way he did. He's so quiet and reserved and grumpy. That last one alone hadn't hinted at the control he'd want in the bedroom.

That's right, baby. Give yourself more pressure. Imagine my cock pumping in and out of you.

I uncross and cross my legs just thinking about his voice through the phone.

I follow that with a deep breath and focus back on my work schedule.

For the next thirty minutes, I alternate between thinking of Simon naked and filling my early mornings with appointments so I can mentally prepare for next week.

After I glanced at the clock for what I can only guess as the fiftieth time in fifteen minutes, I pack up my backpack and then take a shower in the back to get ready. I'll get to Grey's party early, but one of us needs to make the effort to discuss what's happening with us. I guess that someone is going to be me.

I take my time walking home, slowing my steps as Simon's house comes into view.

As I near his driveway, I see there's already a car outside.

Who's here this early? The party doesn't start for another hour. That was supposed to give me plenty of time to pull Simon aside and talk about the other night. Talk about today. We didn't really go into details on how we're going to play this whole fake dating thing. How do we act? I understand fake dating, but Grey will be there. What is too much? What isn't enough? God, I just hope it's someone dropping off cupcakes or something and I still have my chance.

I've made it up one step when Simon comes rushing out.

"Hey, baby," he says, his eyes going wide as he scoops me into a hug. His warm breath hits my ear just as one of the football camp moms comes into view behind him. "She read the invite wrong and showed up early," he whispers into my ear.

I kiss Simon's cheek and hug him back. "You could have texted me a heads up."

He doesn't reply, but he does turn to face the mom behind us, his hand slinking across my lower back to hold me close.

A few things cross my mind in this moment, but the ones I focus on are: is this what Simon would act like if he were really dating someone? Would he greet them like this? Would he hold them against his body possessively the way he is with me right now?

"I'm so sorry," she says and points behind her. "I had Marcus read me the card, and he said noon instead of one, and I just went with it. We're typically early people, but this is a new record for us."

"It's not a problem," Simons assures her. "Marcy—right?"

She nods. "Yes." Then she brushes her hair behind her ear and blushes. "You remembered."

Oh hell. Telling them that we're dating was supposed to kill this kind of behavior. Clearly, I need to turn it up a notch.

I place my hand on Simon's chest and lean into him. "Early doesn't bother us. We're happy to have you."

I kiss his cheek again and step toward Marcy. "Should we go see what the boys are up to while Simon finishes setting up?"

"Oh," Marcy waves a hand. "I'll go check on them so that you can help Simon."

With that, she spins and heads outside.

As soon as I'm sure she's out of earshot, I cross my arms.

"Why didn't you text me?"

"Because." He lets his eyes linger on me a moment longer and then shakes his head. "Shall we?"

He moves past me, but I'm hot on his heels.

"This won't work if you blindside me again."

"I don't plan on blindsiding you again."

"Um, the party starts at one and has no end time. We could be here all night dodging questions."

"Just come up with generic answers as close to the truth."

He reaches into a cabinet to pull out paper plates.

"Sounds so romantic. Should I add in how the first two times we kissed, you stopped it to apologize?"

He turns to face me slowly, a scowl on his face as he crosses his arms.

"I thought we cleared that up."

"Did we?"

"Yes," he answers and continues setting things up on the table.

"Weird, because the only thing I understand right now is your need to hold dominance in the bedro—"

He moves so swiftly, when his hand covers my mouth, you can barely hear my gasp.

"Good. At least we're on the same page for that. As for the other stuff, just wing it. Can you do that?"

I nod.

He removes his hand, and his gaze drops to my lips. He takes a breath and one of his hands brushes my hips.

"Besides," he says, stepping around me. "We don't need to be romantic."

"Simon," I shake my head. "You write romance novels. You know how to be romantic, and it will be a total letdown if you have no romantic skills in real life. No one wants that."

"Perfect." He shuts the cabinet and looks me in the eyes. "Maybe they won't hit on me anymore. Isn't that the whole reason for this plan?"

I hold his gaze and nod. "Well, personally, I'd never date a man who isn't a romantic."

"We aren't dating."

"You're right," I say and step closer. "We're just a couple of neighbors who have phone sex and pretend it never happened."

His eyes go wide and his jaw clenches.

"And those messages are exactly why I didn't warn you," he says in the low tone he used the other night.

"Ha, sure."

I push off the counter, but he reaches his hand out to stop me. His palm meets my stomach, slowly moving to my waist to pull me closer. "I've been avoiding reading them because they're all I can think about. Hell, Greer, if I even looked out my bedroom window this week, all I could hear were your moans. The way my name fell from your lips when you came apart. If I so much as smelled your shampoo or heard your laugh this week, I was imagining all the things I'd do to you if we were alone. If you think I'm pretending it didn't happen, that's because I'm not sure how much longer I can keep my hands to myself. But don't for one second think that I'm pretending it never happened."

I suck in a big breath, my eyes now locked on his lips. With every word he spoke, I swear he leaned closer and closer. He's so close now that I could just twitch, and our lips would be touching.

The images that played in my head that night would become a reality, and I'll never have to dream of what he feels like again. I'll know. I'll go to bed knowing what it felt like to be in his arms without stopping.

His gaze drops to my mouth. I close my eyes, ready for it.

But the front door slams and a voice calls out, "Grey! Grandma is here."

"Shit," Simon says and backs away. "Shit."

"Your parents. Oh my god. Simon," I whisper shout. "What the hell?"

It's Grey's birthday. Of course they're coming. Which means Calla too.

"Too many people will know we're faking it. Oh god. This is bad. This is—"

"So we sell it. We sell it hard, Greer. Please."

I groan.

"Let's just tell everyone the truth. This is too complicated. I want to date for real, not fake date."

He grabs my hand.

"I'll help you then."

"With what?"

"Dating."

"Right, that wouldn't complicate *anything*."

"I'm not saying I'm the guru of dating, Greer, but I do enough research for my books that I could help you. Please, help me. Dating advice, no dating advice—please!"

The panic in his tone stops the words on my lips. I don't have time to ask him about it before his mom and dad step into the kitchen.

"Oh, Simon, hi. Where's Grey?"

Simon waits for my nod. Whatever his reasoning for wanting to fake it for his family, I'll have to wait to find out. All I know from the look in his eyes is he needs this.

"He's in the back with a friend who showed up early," I say and rub Simon's arm as he turns around.

"Speaking of early, you two are as well."

"Well, I was anxious to get here," his mom says. "It's lovely to see you again, Greer."

Her eyes dance between me and her son. Then Simon moves closer to me, and once again rests his hand on my back and on my hip. I swear his mother's eyes pop out.

"What's happening?" she asks and points. "Honey!" She slaps her husband's stomach. "Look!"

She points at us again.

The whole thing catches me so off guard that I laugh.

"Is everything okay?" I ask.

"Are you dating?" his mother says quickly. "Are you dating him?"

"Mom, stop. Yes. Okay. Don't make a big deal of it."

"A big deal?" She gasps. "You've… she's… I… we—"

"Mom," Simon says again and hugs her. "Go find Grey and take a breath."

"And a beer," she says and walks out the door.

Simon's dad chuckles and slaps his son on the shoulder before following her.

We both watch out the window above the sink as they join the others.

Simon lets out the biggest breath I've ever heard and then says, "We started talking once you moved in next door. I'd always had a crush on you as Calla's friend and vice versa, but we never really talked much. Then you started working for me, and we got to know each other. Things happened and, well, suddenly, this is where we are. It's new. We haven't told many people, but it's time because we can't hide our feelings anymore. Does that sound good to you?"

Instead of looking at me, he busies himself with setting up the kitchen with more snacks and drinks. He takes plate after plate from the fridge of burgers, hot dogs, and dressings Grey and I prepped last night before Simon got home.

There's a story here, and later, when we're alone, I'm going to find out what it is.

"Okay." I say. "But you made the first move."

I catch the smallest smile on his lips. "Of course I did."

"I'm irresistible," I say and stroke a finger down his back.

He stiffens, slowly looking over his shoulder. "Now that isn't a lie."

He winks then walks out the back door.

I'm about to follow him, but the front door once again slams shut.

Fast feet rush down the hall, stopping suddenly when they reach the kitchen.

"You're dating my brother?" Calla says on a squeal and then hugs me. "You two are so screwed. I'm not an idiot."

She laughs then hugs her mom, who walks in right as Simon walks out.

"Isn't this the best?" their mom says, and Calla nods.

"It's amazing."

Calla's right. Between lying to Simon's parents and the dent this will put in my chances of actually dating, I'm so totally screwed.

CHAPTER EIGHTEEN
SIMON

I've made a lot of bad choices in my lifetime. I once decided to run a half marathon without training. I wasn't even a runner. I just ran a 5k one weekend and thought *a half marathon can't be that bad.* Spoiler alert. It was. Then there was the time I jumped into the lake in jeans. I was sixteen, so I can't really hold that one against myself. One night in college, I drank so many amaretto sours in a single night to impress a girl that I swear I puked up cherries for three days. So, yeah, the point is, I thought I would be done making poor choices by the time I hit my thirties, but as of right now, that's not the case. Turns out, I still have no idea what I'm doing.

Greer tips her head back on a laugh, her hand reaching out to rest on my mom's shoulder. My mother is laughing just as hard and nodding. She follows it up with swinging arms and a scrunched face. I don't even have to question what story she's telling Greer. Halloween as a kid was my favorite. I took treat-or-treating seriously, and I used the same neighborhood map for six years, thank you very much. Knowing which houses gave out the king-size candy bars was gold for me. I'd have been stupid not to remember them year after year.

"She looks like she's having a good time," Calla says next to me. "Mom has always liked her."

"Who wouldn't?" The words are off my lips before I can stop them. I sip my beer.

"Oh, wow. And here I thought the entire thing was a lie."

"It is."

There's no way Greer and I can fake this from Calla and Beck. For one thing, Grey tells Calla almost anything he can. I bet he's already told her what he did.

"Maybe parts of it, but the part where you like her is totally true."

Of course my sister would find a way to spin this. Yes, Greer is gorgeous, smart, and funny. She's clever and quick-witted, and she loves to keep me on my toes. Grey likes her, and I trust her with him. She's made my life easier the past few weeks, and honestly, I don't know how I can go back to a life that doesn't have her in it on a daily basis. And, yes, I like her, but making it into something more when even I have no idea what's going on isn't a good idea. Calla would get her hopes up, and I can't have that. Among other things.

"Everyone likes Greer. She kind of makes it hard not to."

"Mm-hmm. You *really* like her."

"Calla, stop."

"Oh come on, Simon. You're a grown man. You can have feelings for someone. It's normal. Actually, it would be abnormal if you never had feelings. I like Greer. She'd be good for you. I'm just trying to figure out why you two are in this little arrangement. Getting Mom to stop bugging you about dating, I get. What does Greer get? How does this work out for her?"

She gets dating advice to use with someone else.

Fuck.

Did I really offer that to her?

"If we ever actually date, I'll keep in mind that you approve. How does that sound?"

"Like fun Simon had a prior engagement and sent grumpy Simon to his kid's birthday party."

I let out a hmph and step off the back porch toward my mother and Greer. Mom is starting to get really animated, so it's best to cut them off now and steal Greer away.

Outside of that moment in the kitchen, we haven't had much alone time together. If we're going to put on a show, we should probably be near one another, right? Then again, maybe we're doing just fine being in our element and not making a show of it. Because despite the fact we would be faking it, every touch and every kiss I'd give her—those would be real.

I pause and look around the yard for Grey, spotting him and his friends shouting out *dead or alive* with a football.

I smile, thinking of the day the guys and I taught him that game.

"Coach Blue!" Grey calls out and tosses the ball in the air. "You made it."

He runs to him, his teammates following behind. They each give the coach a fist bump before going back to their game.

I walk over and extend my hand. "Glad you could make it."

"Yeah." He rubs his chin. "I don't do a lot of parties with

my camp kids, but since Grey is going to try out at school in the fall and I'll be coaching him, I figured this could be an exception. Plus, this group of boys is one of my best." He scans the yard, skimming over the table and chairs and the boys. Then he stops and grins.

Greer.

Came here for the kids, my ass. He's here to see Greer.

Go figure.

"Well, there's food and drinks in the kitchen. Just that way." I point away from Greer, but his eyes never stray as he nods.

"Yeah, I'll grab some in a minute. Thanks for the invite. I'm going to go mingle."

As soon as he starts walking toward Greer, something inside of me snaps.

She isn't mine, but she sure as hell isn't his.

"Simon!" Tobias yells from my back door as he holds it open to let Natalie through. "I have news."

I hold a finger up, watching as Coach Blue strides up to Greer and pulls her attention from my parents.

Without thinking too much about it, I take a few quick strides, stepping up next to Greer and sliding my hand along her lower back to pull her close. Then, as if I'm on autopilot, I kiss the top of her head.

"I'm going inside to chat with Tobias for a few minutes, but I wanted to check on you real fast," I say as she twists into me, resting her hand on my chest.

Our gazes lock. We might be faking it for prying eyes, but the smile she gives me and the coy look in her eyes is very real.

"Oh, you're so sweet. I'm okay. I'll be right behind you. Walker just wanted to ask me something real quick."

Oh, I bet he fucking did. And when the hell did these two get on a first-name basis?

"Oh, what's that?" I ask.

"I don't know yet," she says.

We both turn to him, waiting.

"Oh, I didn't know that the two of you were together. I thought you were just watching Grey to help out."

"That's how it started, but look at her," I say and do just that. I swear my breath catches when she looks at me. "Her beauty may have caught my eye first, but getting to know her has been a gift, and I wasn't about to let that go."

Greer bites her bottom lip, never taking her focus off me.

Hell. I know how sweet that lip tastes. I'm jealous she gets to bite it anytime she wants. Right now, I'm tempted to do it myself. Put myself out of this misery and give myself what has been on my mind day and night for the past week.

To say I've been the master of control the past seven days is an understatement. Each day she showed up in one of those spandex sport dress things and converse sneakers, that control snapped a little more. And today, now that I get to touch her freely and act as if she were really mine, I can't make any promises.

I'm not sure how much time has passed before Coach Blue clears his throat.

As much as it pains me, I pull my gaze from Greer's.

"Sorry. You had a question?"

"Oh, um, yeah, it was just… I was just checking to see if Grey mentioned needing new shoes. His are getting pretty worn, and I recommended a couple of brands for the fall school year."

Shoes. Ha.

"We'll be sure to get them for him," I say.

"Thank you for reminding me. I did, in fact, forget to mention that to Simon this week," Greer adds in a much more polite tone than the one I'd been using. I can't help it.

Until this afternoon, I never put a second thought into Greer talking or flirting or even dating another guy. I don't like it. Not one bit.

"Of course. Well, I better go grab some of that food you mentioned."

"Bye, Walker." Greer waits just till he's out of earshot and whispers, "Playing the jealous boyfriend a little strong, aren't we?"

I pin her with a look. "There was no playing about it, Greer," I say and then lean in as close as I can get. I'm so close, my lips brush her cheek as I speak. "We might not be dating for real, but something is going on between us, and until we have out the details, the only man who should be getting your attention is me."

I pull back to see heat in her eyes. They glance to my lips, and I give her what she wants. I kiss her right here in my backyard despite the fact that my family could be watching, or anyone else for that matter. I don't care. What I do care about, however, is anyone getting to see the glow on her face when she's turned on. That's only for me.

So I break the kiss and tell her, "And yes, until we figure this out, the only woman who matters to me is you."

Her chest rises on an inhale, and I smirk.

"Do you like when I claim you?"

"Okay!" Calla says next to us. "I'm not sure what's happening here, but a little breathing room at an eleven-year-old's party would be appropriate."

My sister puts her arms between us and wiggles between us until I finally step back.

"Before I forget," my mother says, joining us, "Greer, you must come to dinner next weekend in Melody. Simon, you'll bring her?"

"Yes," I say before Greer can come up with an excuse.

She glares and shakes her head at me, but there's a faint smile on her lips.

"That would be lovely, Mrs. Stone. Thank you."

"Of course. I can't wait!" Mom claps and then shouts. "Let's open presents."

All the kids hustle into the house while I keep Greer right by my side.

I keep my attention on Greer PG-rated for the remainder of the party, but the next time I get her alone, all bets are off.

CHAPTER NINETEEN
GREER

If anyone were to ask me if I avoided Simon and his house on Sunday, I'd tell them yes.

Not that I didn't take a peek from time to time from my bedroom window like a weirdo. After all, it wasn't like I just stood there waiting for him. No. If I was in my room, I'd look.

I never saw him.

It's for the best.

I also never texted him, and he never texted me. Truth be told, I thought he might reach out. I'm fully aware that we told everyone we're fake dating, but it didn't feel fake. Not one bit of it did.

What the hell does this mean?

I lean back in my chair at the studio and press my palms into my eyes.

I thought this Monday morning would be a welcome distraction.

I was wrong.

I have one more client until I go hang out with Grey for

the afternoon, and as excited as I am to see Simon, I'm equally as nervous.

I close my planner, then stand to stretch and lay out equipment for Harvey, my next client. Harvey is always trying to set me up with his son, and I always decline. I can't date clients or their family members. It would more than likely end up being bad for business. At least today I have an excuse, but honestly, how long can Simon and I keep this up? It's been a whole two days of pretending and my stress level has me rearranging my schedule for an extra yoga session this week.

Just as I'm finished laying out a couple of yoga mats, my watch buzzes. It's a notification from Harvey. He needs to cancel.

Perfect.

I sigh and then put away everything I just laid out. Then I grab the vacuum and clean the floors, making sure to take the handle piece off and get all the edges. Next, I wipe down the kettle bells, the mats, the hand weights, the chair in front of my desk, and then I do the windows. After that, I clean up my desk and make a smoothie, then check my calendar for tomorrow. Grey is coming with me tomorrow afternoon, and I have some fun things planned for us. He doesn't know it yet, but I carved out a half hour just for him. So we can do the exercise he wants specifically. It's not something I do for most clients, but I do understand the need to want your workout to be fun. If you don't enjoy it, you won't stick to it, and I want Grey to keep this up. I think he wants to keep it up, so I'm here to help.

But right now, my nose is itching from the smell of disinfectant. I let out a long breath and grab my things, pushing my bike out the door and locking up.

The summer sun warms my body instantly, and I soak it up. This season never lasts long.

I check my watch once more.

I'll be close to two hours early if I go home now. I know that Simon is on a deadline, so perhaps he'd appreciate that I'm early. On the other hand, that leaves me with more time around him, and as much as I want that, I'm not so sure it's a good idea.

There's a line drawn between us, and to be frank, we both just flat out ignore it. We see it, but it's blurry. As much as I want to care that we don't cross it again, I don't. Simon makes me feel different. He makes me feel like someone actually sees me.

Go figure. The first man to make me feel like there are still men out there who can make you feel like their whole world, and he's faking it.

But it feels so real.

I shake my head and get on my bike, pedaling home. It makes no sense to sit around and think of the what ifs. Simon and I need to figure this out.

If I get there now, we'll have plenty of time to do just that whether he likes it or not. Besides, I know why we're faking it for the football moms, but what about his family? Why fake it for them? I have too many questions I should have asked over the weekend. But whenever I'm alone with Simon, it's like my brain short-circuits.

Don't even get me started on how I'm supposed to take dating advice from him later. At this point, even if he's some long-lost twin of Simon's who talks and acts just like him, I don't want him.

I head toward our houses and as soon as a trickle of sweat

starts to form between my breasts from the ninety-degree July heat, I pedal faster. This would be a great time to drive my new car and turn the AC on, but fresh air has always been a way for me to calm my mind, plus, I like riding my bike. I swear it's a form of therapy. I could never live somewhere that couldn't make this possible.

I round the final corner, a smile on my face because Simon sitting outside writing is a sight to see. It's like this secret thing we have in common. Using the air as motivation to do what we love.

But today I don't see him.

I slow in front of his house and stare at his writing spot.

When has Simon not been out here when I get home?

Something is off.

I hop off my bike, letting it drop to the ground instead of taking the time to put the kickstand up, and jog up the steps. The front door is unlocked.

All the lights inside are turned off.

Not super unusual for the middle of the day, since the sun shining through the windows lights up the room, but still, I can just feel something is wrong. I don't hear Grey's TV or anyone in the kitchen or even music downstairs where Simon could be working or working out. I tiptoe into the kitchen and glance at the coffeepot.

It's still clean. There's always at least once cup left by the time I get here.

I spin quickly and run up the stairs. I stop at Grey's room first. He isn't there, but all his sheets have been stripped off his bed. Slowly, I move to Simon's room. The door is cracked, but immediately, I see both him and Grey in bed.

I push the door open, and my eyes fall to the medicine on the nightstand and the thermometer next to it.

Oh, Grey must be sick.

I touch a hand to my heart as I slowly back up. Simons clearly doesn't need…

Simon groans and rolls over, the very obvious sweat running off his forehead tells me all I need to know.

They're *both* sick.

I walk back into the room and put a hand to Simon's forehead. He's hot. I don't need to take his temperature to know that he's running a fever.

I do the same to Grey—he's even hotter.

My mind instantly goes into list mode of what I need. Water, check their temps so I can track when they start to go down, get more medicine, start some soup, get them clean sheets, grab my heating pad, and —

Grey bolts up, leaning over the edge of the bed and throwing up. I run to do who knows what for him, and then I see the trash can by the bed.

"Grey," Simon says with a hoarse voice. "Let me get you some more crackers."

He starts to move, but I put a hand on his ankle.

"Don't move. I'll get it."

"Greer?" Simon says, then groans and falls back onto the pillow. "You should go. You don't want this."

"Maybe not." I head for the door. "But I'm here, and I'm not leaving. Don't either of you move until I get back."

"Greer, you don't need to take care of us. I can do this. I've done it before on my own, and I'll do it again, sick or not."

He sits up, so I march right back into the bedroom. I place a hand on his shoulder to gently push him back down.

"I know you can, Simon, but those were your pre-Greer days. You're stuck with me now. Sick or not. Now lay back down. I'll be right back."

He doesn't say anything. He just gazes into my eyes, then gives a slight nod.

"All right then," I say.

By the time I make it back to the room, both of them are asleep again.

I know this isn't the time to think this, but damn, seeing Simon snuggle his son has my ovaries working overtime. He's an amazing dad, and that quality is just one of many about Simon that turns me on.

Damnit.

I don't want to catch feelings for Simon. Yes, I can be attracted to him and want to fool around, but real feelings aren't good. He's never once mentioned wanting to settle down. Not ever.

Which, clearly, is the exact opposite of what I want.

But maybe he just needed to find the right woman.

Maybe that woman could be me?

CHAPTER TWENTY
SIMON

I feel like an elephant is sitting on my head and a lion used my throat as a scratching post.

I hate being sick. It's the absolute worst thing ever. No, scratch that. Seeing my son sick is the worst thing ever.

Grey!

My eyes spring open, but it isn't Grey who I see next to me in bed. Nope. It's Greer. Greer propped next to me reading my last release. She flips a page, her hand touching her bottom lips as she takes a deep breath.

She hasn't noticed that I'm awake, so I take a moment to study her while she reads. Her lips smile softly, and I swear she pulls the book closer, her eyes scanning the words as if she's trying to set a world record for reading. Her hair is pulled into a messy bun, little pieces falling out to frame her face. The pink gloss on her lips is nothing short of distracting.

I scan lower, taking in the low vee dip of her olive-green sleeveless tank top. Her legs are under the covers, so I can't see anything else.

She's gorgeous, and every time I look at her, it's as if my mind can't believe this woman actually enjoys being near me. Could actually want to kiss me. Want to be with me. My heart warms. Seeing her as soon as I woke up, it feels right.

But she deserves someone who can give her forever.

Even when my mind says I'm not allowed to think that, I do.

I just don't know what to do about it. Or if I even should.

"What page are you on?" I ask, and she startles, tossing the book out in front of her.

"What? I don't know."

I chuckle, pushing up to a seated position and glancing at the clock.

"Fuck, Greer, it's five in the afternoon. Where's Grey? Did we sleep all day?"

I start to toss my leg over the edge, but she stops me.

"Stay here. He's fine. His fever broke around three, and he's downstairs watching TV and eating some chicken noodle soup."

I run my hand over my face. I slept through the entire day when he needed me. How did I let that happen?

"I can get you a bowl if you're feeling up to it."

"You made soup?"

She nods.

"I don't think I'm ready for food. But I need to get up and get things done."

"You just need to rest," she says next to me, and once again, pushes me back to sit.

"And here I thought you liked when I was in control" are the words that fall from my lips.

Her eyes meet mine, and she smirks. "Not today."

I reach for her, but she smacks my hand away.

"Clearly, you're feeling better."

"I am. But like I said, I have things to do."

"You really don't. I already finished washing Grey's sheets and remade his bed and then sanitized the house. I made soup, and I even have fresh sheets ready for your bed when you do get up, which is not right this minute. I cleaned as I normally do too."

She keeps listing the things she did today, but it all starts to blur. It's been so long since I had someone take care of me the way she has today. The way she clearly took care of Grey. It's obvious that once she told me she was here, my body shut down.

I trust Greer more than I want to. I feel for Greer more than I want to. We might be faking the dating storyline, but the feelings I'm developing for Greer are very real.

"Thank you," I say as soon as she stops talking. "I'm happy that you're here."

This time, she doesn't swat my hand away when I reach for it.

"If I get sick, you better take care of me," she says. "After all, I did clean out Grey's vomit bucket, sooooo you don't get a choice."

I laugh and nod. "It's a deal."

"Good."

She leans forward and grabs the book she'd been reading.

"This is really good," she says, looking over the cover and then at the back. Her hand runs over the words. "I like this finish. It's so soft. If all books had this, I'd be broke."

"I like it too."

"Before I bought my house, the Realtor told me that it was vacant for a while. Did that inspire this series?"

I reach for the book, smiling at my own work. No matter how many times I look at them, anytime I see my books in print, I can't help but be happy and thankful how some parts of my life worked out exactly how I wanted.

"Yep. After the first month went by and the house didn't sell, I wondered why, and somewhere that morphed into this series."

"I like how you have this whole town secret for the house that's pieced together in each couple's books. How many books will I have to read before I find out the truth behind this mysterious house?"

I smirk. "Greer Harrison, are you telling me that you've read the first four books in this series?"

She smiles with pride and nods once. "I sure am. I'm a secret fan."

"I had no idea."

She turns to look at me, both our heads resting back on the headboard.

"You're an amazing writer, Simon. You have a gift."

"Thank you."

"Plus, I can relate to the heroine in this book. I know what it's like to be so lonely that even when red flags are painted on your forehead, you push ahead because you want to see the good in everyone."

I reach for her hand.

The words are on my lips, but nothing comes out.

I don't want to be another red flag for her, but I just *can't* give her what she wants.

When I finally muster the courage to say something, anything, Grey appears in the doorway.

He crosses his arms and laughs.

Greer quickly scrambles out of the bed. "Do you need something?"

I'm not sure if her reaction is from Grey seeing us or if she is actually worried about him.

"I'm fine." He steps into the room and points at me. "I can't believe you're still in bed. What a wimp," he teases.

He laughs again, but then his face turns green, and he runs to the bathroom. Greer is hot on his heels and gets to him before I can.

She's rubbing his back and whispering soothing words to him. Something inside me snaps.

If I don't figure my shit out now, some other lucky bastard is going to swoop in and take this wonderful woman from me.

CHAPTER TWENTY-ONE
GREER

"I feel sick."

"No, you don't," Simon tells me as soon as he meets me out on his front porch. It's been an entire week since I found him and Grey sick. Now, we're heading to his parents' house for a Friday night family dinner, and I think it's my turn to puke.

"Really. Do I feel hot?"

He puts his hand on my forehead.

"Not even a little."

"Well, I think I caught what you had. I better just go back to my house and—"

"It's going to be fine."

"I don't like lying to your parents."

I feel like a bad person. Maybe if I knew the reason why he wants to do this, I'd feel better. The real reason. Not the "so that my mom will stop asking me" generic reason Simon gave me earlier this week.

Seems fitting enough, but there's something he's not telling me.

"It's fine. It's a small lie. Besides"—he pauses to watch Grey head back inside the house before he steps up close to me— "not everything about what we're saying is a lie, right?"

This would be the perfect moment for him to kiss me. Sneak one in real quick. But he doesn't. In fact, all week he's been nothing but a gentleman to me. There have been no tempting moments between us. Not even one.

It seems that maybe he has made up his mind.

We all load into the truck and are soon off on our way to Simon's parents in Melody. It's a short trip, only a couple of hours, and before I know it, we're pulling up in front of their house. The house is cute: the curved driveway, the newly painted brick siding, the way each tree is planted perfectly to line the driveway and give what little privacy they can get from the main road. But what keeps drawing my attention is his sister's car is parked in front of us.

"I didn't know Calla and Beck were coming," I say, and I unclick my belt.

Grey has already jumped out of the truck and is running to where his grandma smiles in front of the white front door.

"It's a family dinner, Greer. Of course she's here."

"I know. Of course I knew that. It's just—"

Play the part. It's just one more night.

I blow out a breath and nod.

"Let's do this."

We both get out, meeting in front of Simon's truck.

He grabs my hand, lacing our fingers, and then leans down to whisper in my ear.

"Thank you again for doing this."

I nod. He kisses my temple. His mom swoons from the front step.

So far, so good.

Hand in hand, we move toward the house, and his mom pulls me into the biggest and tightest hug I've ever had.

"This is such a wonderful night. A full house. I love it."

"Oh, well, isn't it the lovely new couple?" Calla says as soon as we walk into the dining room. She's playing cards with her dad, Beck, and now Grey. "Holding hands.'" She puts a hand on her heart and sighs. "It's just too cute."

"I agree." His mom pops out from the kitchen with a homemade charcuterie board. "It makes my heart so happy to see you with someone."

As if Simon knew her words were going to make me squirm, he removes his hand from mine and wraps it around my shoulders, causing me to turn into him.

"Cool it, Mom. You keep saying things like that and you'll scare her away."

"Yeah, that's what's going to make her run." Beck laughs. "Of all the things."

"Stop teasing him," Simon's dad says. "He's a grown man and can make his own choices."

"Thank you, Dad," Simon says, releasing me.

Calla points to the cards. "Do you two want to play?"

"What game is it?" I ask.

"Bullshit!" Grey shouts loud enough for all of us to jump.

I laugh while Simon shakes his head. "You couldn't have picked any other game?"

"It's his favorite," Calla defends Grey. "Besides, I smell a whole lot of bullsh—"

"We'll play," I cut in before she can finish.

I take a seat, and Simon takes the one next to me, scooting over until our chairs are touching, and placing his arm on the back of my chair. Then he twists his hat backward, leans toward me, and says, "I hope you're good at this game, because I win almost every match."

"*Almost* being the keyword," Beck says. "Till I joined the family."

"Speaking of joining the family," his mom says, and she sits by his dad. "Greer, should we move your seat at the reception next to Simon's?"

Calla grins like the Cheshire cat.

"Yes, we should."

"Can you explain it to me again? Why are you having a party and not a wedding?" Grey asks, looking at Calla and Beck.

"Because they're already married."

"But when?"

"That's a story for another day," Simon cuts in. "Let's play."

* * *

Games and good food with great company. I couldn't have imagined a better Friday night.

I cup my tea, letting the hot water keep my hands warm as Calla, Mrs. Stone, and I all sit on the back porch. Grey, Beck, Simon, and his dad are all in the yard playing football. It's a chillier summer night, but still, it's one of the better ones I've had in a long time.

Being with Simon's family has been more than I could ask for. I'd forgotten what it was like to be around family. To see their interactions and their love for each other. This is exactly why I want a real boyfriend. So that eventually I can have moments in my life just like this one, but it's weird. Now that I'm here, I can't imagine having something different.

But it will be different. Because this isn't real. No matter what kind of attraction Simon and I have, I can't forget that. After tonight, unless his family comes around, I don't see why we would need to continue faking it.

Which would then bring us to a day when the guy I'm crushing on gives me dating advice for another man.

God, I'm a mess.

"He really loves that sport, doesn't he?" Simon's mom asks.

"He does. Grey's really good too. Some of the other moms at camp are always talking about how gifted he is, but I think he was just raised to do his best when it comes to something he loves."

"I bet you do," Calla says and sips her own tea.

I cast a look in her direction, and she nods to the house.

"I need more tea," she says.

"I'll come with you," I say.

Once we're in the kitchen, she starts to warm up some water on the stove. Then she moves to the kitchen island, resting her forearms on it.

"So, how long do you think you and my brother can pull off this fake dating show of yours?"

I take a breath and step back as if she slapped me.

"What?"

"Come on, Greer." She laughs. "You and my brother, it would never work. Plus, that night Grey spent the night before his party, he told Beck and I what happened at camp. We just didn't think you two would actually keep it up."

I debate it for a moment and then sigh.

"It was an accident. I didn't think Simon would have to know, and I didn't think anyone was going to get involved." I point over my shoulder to her mom. "I don't want anyone to get hurt."

The back door opens as I'm pointing, and Simon walks in.

"What are you two doing?" he asks. His question has some annoyance to it as he looks at his sister.

"Just talking, Simon. Calm down."

His gaze shifts to me and every feature in his face softens.

"Grey is apparently spending the weekend here now. Are you ready to head back?"

"Just us?" I ask even though it's clear that's exactly what he meant.

"Yep." He tucks a strand of hair behind my ear and then presses the softest of kisses to my lips.

"Seriously?" Calla groans and walks out.

I should tell him that she knows, and he doesn't have to fake it in front of her, but I don't. At this point, I'm taking anything I can get from Simon.

Eventually, I'll find the man who will want to make a life with me.

And no matter how much my heart is falling for him, it won't be Simon.

I just need a little longer to come to terms with it.

CHAPTER TWENTY-TWO
SIMON

I needed an excuse to kiss Greer. Which is exactly why I'd kissed her in front of my sister, even knowing my sister knew the truth. I'll handle my sister later when she will no doubt question me about it, but I'd been watching Greer all night with my family, and just like Monday when I woke up to her next to me in my bed, it felt right.

Everything about her being here with me is right.

But like all the times before, this part of me, the dark part, says I can't have it.

I steal a glance her way as we drive down the road. She hasn't spoken much since we left, but I just chalked it up to the fact that my mom asked her every single question known to man in just under four hours. I'm not exaggerating either. I officially know that Greer was vaccinated as a kid. Yep. My mom asked that. I told Greer she didn't need to answer, but she seemed to love everything about the inquisition.

"Are you okay?" I ask after a few more minutes of silence.

She nods.

"Okay."

"Actually, no. What's the real reason you wanted me there tonight? And don't say it's so your mom will stop asking you about a girlfriend. You're a grown man, Simon. You can just tell her you don't have one."

I suck in a breath, my eyes on the road. She's not wrong, but how much do I tell her?

"I want the truth this time."

And she deserves it. After all, she's been helping me all summer, and outside of a paycheck, what have I ever done for her?

"I…" is all I get out before the words get stuck.

I clear my throat, ready to try again, but Greer speaks first.

"You don't have to tell me. I just—"

"I do want to tell you. I'm just not used to sharing this with a lot of people."

"Please don't feel like you have to share it with me."

"I want to."

She waits for me to find my words again.

"When Grey's mom died, I…"

It's like my body knows that telling Greer will change things. There won't be anything left to tell her after I do this.

Greer reaches over to hold my free hand.

"It's a pain I don't want to experience again, and it's a pain I'd never wish on someone. Dating means taking that chance for both parties, and as for tonight, I wanted to give my mom some sort of happiness in this area of my life. Even if it's not going to last."

Considering Greer's mindset is the total opposite of mine,

I hold my breath, waiting for the moment when she pulls her hand from mine.

When she finally shuts me out and ends this thing between us.

But she doesn't move her hand, and I slowly turn to catch her watching me. Greer and I have spent a lot of time together this summer, and at this point, I can usually read her mind, but right now, I don't even know where to begin.

I can hear the faint music playing from my car stereo as I wait for her to say something. I know I stumbled through my words at first. Maybe when they finally came out, they were too much for her.

She blinks, and a tear drops from her eye.

"Don't do that," I say. "Please don't cry for me."

She shakes her head and swipes the tear away. "I'm not. It's just… I think you're one of the best dads, brothers, sons, friends I've ever met, and to know that you think you…" Her words trail off as she shakes her head. "Now I know why you keep pushing me away when we kiss."

"I promise I'm not trying to hurt you."

"Can I ask you something?" she asks as if she didn't hear my last statement.

"Of course."

"When do you think about yourself?"

"What?"

She twists in her seat, pulling one leg up to tuck the ankle under her other knee. She's ready to have a good talk, and we still have at least an hour to go. I should have known anything I said wouldn't scare her.

This is *Greer*.

There is no one like her.

"I mean, genuinely, when was the last time you didn't think of others, and you did what you wanted?"

I rub my chin and grin. "The night we had phone sex."

"Mm-hmm, that doesn't count."

"Really? Because I'm pretty sure I did what I wanted that night, consequences be damned."

The conversation we're having now should have been one we had before that night, but I can't go back now, and I sure as hell don't regret that night either.

"Come on, Simon, be serious."

I sigh. "I don't know. My life has been pretty crazy lately."

"Okay, well, if you could do one thing right now, if you could drive this car anywhere, where would you choose?"

"I really don't know."

"Simon."

"How about, I'll think about it and let you know when we get home?"

She crosses her arms and pretends to pout, but after only a few seconds, she says, "You better think of something."

The conversation steers away from anything serious to the way Grey yelled bullshit and how Beck didn't win a single hand tonight. I learn that Greer once found a dog on the side of the road, hid it in her room, feeding him table scraps until she felt so bad that she finally called the number on his collar so he could go back to his family.

"I still can't believe you gave him back. Weren't you in love with him by then? Pets are the easiest to love."

"Oh, it was super hard, but my mom came home and had the next day off, and I knew she'd find him eventually."

"She didn't all the other nights?"

"No, she worked a lot, so by the time she'd come home, she usually just said good night and was half-asleep when she did it."

That was another thing I learned tonight. Greer grew up with only her mom.

"How many jobs did your mom work?"

"Three. Most days she pulled doubles."

"Did you see her often? That sounds like she would never be home."

"It was definitely few and far between some days, but I never felt alone with her. And her days off were my favorite. We'd sleep in, watch a movie, order pizza, then go get ice cream. We didn't have much, but I didn't need much as long as I had her."

Fuck. Greer's heart is so kind, she doesn't need a man like me in her life. One who can't commit out of fear. She deserves better.

We take turns singing the chorus of songs from Journey to Blake Shelton and before I know it, I'm pulling into my driveway.

"Thanks again for coming tonight."

"Of course. You mom really was happy."

I nod. "I suppose we'll need to think of a reason to split up."

"Yeah, but let's wait till the end of the summer." She winks at me. "I'd like to keep my job and all."

I laugh as she takes a step backward, waving goodbye.

I follow her. "If you think I'm not going to walk you to your door after everything you've done for me then you don't know me very well."

"Oh, I knew you would," she says and bumps my arms with hers.

We reach her door, and I lean against the frame while she unlocks it. As soon as the door opens, I push off, twist my hat backward, ready to tell her goodnight, but then she leans against the opposite side of the door and looks up at me.

Her gaze drops to my mouth the way mine does to hers.

"Well, I—"

"Why don't you come inside?" she asks, reaching for the waist of my jeans and tugging me. "And stay."

I let out a groan as she tilts her face up to me, her lips dangerously close to mine.

"You still want me to come inside after everything I just told you in the car?"

"Yeah." She kisses my lips. "I do."

This is it. My moment. When I can finally have her. When we both know where we stand.

I'm not pushing her away this time.

I cradle her head in my hands as I crash my lips to hers. Her hands move frantically to grip my shirt as we stumble backward into her house.

She flicks the light on and closes the door, never taking her lips off mine. I reach down, gripping her by the back of her thighs and lift her until her legs wrap around me.

"Fuck, Greer. Is this really happening?"

"Yes." She moans, pulling away to fumble with my belt as I hold her. "My room is upstairs."

"Oh, trust me. I know where it's at."

By the time I make it to her room, my belt has been left behind somewhere and my jeans are unbuttoned. She drops to her feet and grins up at me, reaching up to touch my hat.

"Whatever you do," she says softly, "keep this hat just the way it is."

"You got it." I take a step back and unzip my pants, pulling my shirt over my head. I do my best not to disturb the hat.

She takes a deep breath.

"Wow."

I smirk and then widen my stance and cross my arms.

"I'm half naked. It's time that you are too."

Ever so slowly, she spins and takes a step backward.

"Can you unzip me?"

Her sweet smell surrounds me as my hand brushes her smooth, warm skin.

Greer Harrison is about to get naked for me. Me. Simon Stone.

The thought that I don't deserve this creeps into my mind, so I shake it away.

Tonight, I do. Tonight, she does. If this is my only chance with her, I'm going to make it one we both remember for the rest of our lives.

She shimmies out of her dress, and it drops to the ground; all I can focus on is this gorgeous woman in front of me. Especially the bare skin of her perfect butt.

"Remove that too," I say and nod to the black thong she's wearing.

She blushes but does what she's told.

My eyes scan her from head to toe, my cock jumping at the thought of what's going to happen. Of that moment when I'm inside her and my name is the only word that falls from her lips.

"Now what?" she asks, standing in front of me completely bare.

I smile. "Do you like being told what to do?"

I brush my hand along her cheek before my lips descend on hers.

"Only by you," she whispers.

That's my snapping point.

I swoop one hand behind her to lift her as I spin to sit on the bed. She lands on my lap, legs straddling me.

She balances herself with her hands on my shoulder, pressing herself against me. She starts to sway her hips, but I grip them tight and stop her.

"I didn't tell you that you could do that."

"What am I supposed to do?"

I lean back, resting on my elbows for the briefest moment. "You crawl over me and sit on my face."

Her eyes widen as she bites her lip, failing to hide the smile on her lips.

I lay back, and she complies. I don't waste any time tasting her.

I take one slow lick against her core.

"Fuck."

"What?" she asks on a gasp.

"You taste delicious, Greer. How the hell have I kept myself from this?"

And how the hell am I going to stay away from it after tonight?

She answers me with a moan.

Her hips buck at the next swipe, so I reach up, each hand cupping an ass cheek.

"Hold on the edge of the bed," I tell her.

I feast as if I'm a starved man and this is my last meal. To be honest, if it were, I'd be a happy man.

"Oh god, Simon."

Her words fuel me to quicken my pace. I remove one hand from her ass to slip a finger inside of her.

Like before, she tries to bend her back.

"Oh my god. I've never… this has never…"

Does it make me a sadist that I enjoy the fact she can't finish a sentence right now? That my face between her legs has her so goddamn flustered that she can't think straight?

Hell, I'm not a sadist, I'm just a man who wants to make this woman come harder than she ever has before.

"Simon, I'm... I'm…"

I can feel her begin to pulse around my finger, so I pull out and sit up, holding on to her.

I flip her to her back, spreading her legs wider. She's splayed out in front of me, ready to orgasm.

I'm the man who gets to do that for her.

"Simon!" she groans and threads one hand through her hair. "I was almost there."

"I know, baby, but when you come for the first time tonight, it's going to be with my cock inside you. Got it?"

She sucks in a breath on a nod.

"Now, hold your hands above your head and do not touch anything unless I tell you that you can."

The glow in her eyes is all I need to know that she wants to be commanded as much as I want to command her.

I move off the bed to strip off the remainder of my clothes. Greer's gaze falls immediately to my cock as it bounces free from my boxers.

I grip it and stroke.

"You did this to me. Do you like knowing that?"

She nods.

"Good."

I grab a gold foil packet from my wallet and slide it on. I grin down at her as she licks her lips.

Fuck. I didn't think I could get harder.

I crawl over, nudging her legs apart to sit myself between them. I line myself up to her, but instead of pushing in, I tease her in up and down strokes, letting her wetness coat me.

"God, you're fucking beautiful, Greer. But looking at you like this, hell, I don't know how I haven't lost control yet."

"Do it. Lose control. As far as I'm concerned," she says, her voice deep, seductive, and matching the tone I've been using on her, "we have the entire weekend for you to take it slow."

An entire weekend… with Greer?

Hell, I won't turn that down.

And as much as I love to take control, I'm going to give her what she wants. Lord knows it's exactly what I want too.

I slowly push in.

"Yessss," she breathes, her head tilting back. Her hands have moved from above her head to threading through her hair again, and I love that I make her this crazy.

I push in another inch, and her back bows, angling so that she can take more of me.

"God, that feels…"

"Like heaven," I finish for her and slam all the way home.

My hand finds hers to hold as the other braces my body above hers.

"Hold on, baby, I'm about to give you what you want."

I pull back slowly and slam into her again. And again.

And again. When her moans grow louder, I silence them with my mouth. I love listening to her, but if she doesn't have an outlet for the feeling I'm giving her, then it'll increase tenfold, and right now, the only thing I want her to feel is me. All of me.

I slip my tongue past her lips to meet hers, the tempo of those strokes matching my hips.

She breaks the kiss.

"Simon, Simon!"

"That's right, come for me. Come all over me. Milk me until I see stars, Greer."

Nothing about what I just said logically makes sense, but as soon as my dick feels her contract around me, my vision blacks out and the stars I'd been asking her for fill my eyes.

I come so hard that my hips are still moving, thinking they are in for round two, long after she's regained her breath.

When my mind calms and I can see the woman lying under me, smiling as if I'm her world, I know that this weekend, there is nowhere else I'd rather be.

If you could do any one thing in this world without thinking of others, what would it be?

To spend as much time with Greer as I can.

Consequences be damned.

CHAPTER TWENTY-THREE
GREER

I'm not crazy, okay.

I know how this looks. The girl who can't wait to fall in love invites the man who made it clear he doesn't want to date into her bed.

Do I think I can change him? No. But it wouldn't feel right to let him go on thinking that being alone for the rest of your life is better than heartbreak.

For one weekend, I want to give him what he thinks he can't have or doesn't deserve.

I can't compare my life to his, but I have to at least show him what he can have. Even if he doesn't want it with me.

Plus, it feels really, *really* nice to be wanted. I haven't felt this in years. Call me selfish. I don't care.

This weekend is for us, for different reasons, and I'm not going to regret a single moment of it.

I can feel the sunlight peeking its way through my window, but I haven't opened my eyes yet. Instead, I'm pretending to sleep while a very warm body behind me draws a circle on my back.

Waking up next to someone feels like I can breathe a little.

Like this dream I have might not be so far away after all. Like I still have a chance.

If only that dream could be with Simon.

"I know you're awake," Simon says and then kisses my shoulder.

"Am I?" I say, still not opening my eyes.

He chuckles, and the sound calls to me to roll over and face him.

"Hi."

Instead of replying, he leans forward and kisses me.

Unlike our kisses last night, this morning his lips are soft against mine, and they take their time. He reaches for my hips and tugs me until our bodies are chest to chest.

I feel his morning erection and moan into the kiss.

I let my hand sneak under the sheets between us, taking him in my hand.

Simon likes to sleep naked, and you will hear no complaints from me on this fun fact.

"Greer," he groans.

I ignore him, letting my hand slowly stroke him.

"Fuck," he breaths out, growing harder in my hand.

"I would have thought you'd be too tired today," I whisper against his lips, twisting my body until I'm half on him, with one leg resting between his knees.

"When it comes to you, it seems there's no such thing as too much."

"Good," I say, pressing a kiss on his cheek before scooting down on the bed. "Because there is something I've been waiting to do ever since I watched you take your clothes off last night."

"You don't—"

I lick up the length of his cock.

Look, I know he's big, all right? I felt him more than once last night, and each time, I swore he wouldn't fit, but he did. Somehow my body just made room for him—from my bed to the couch in my living room to when he bent me over my dresser to when we showered before we finally fell asleep. He fit as if he were made for me.

My mouth, on the other hand—I'm not sure I can even get half of him in there.

I lick every side of him, making sure to circle my tongue over the tip until there's enough of my mouth to create lube for my hand. The parts that won't fit need attention, too, and I'm going to make sure they get it.

"Fuck, Greer," he says, his hands finding my hair and tugging. "That feels great."

If that feels great, imagine what he's going to say in just a second.

Eager to find out, I lower my mouth around him and take him as deep as I can.

"Holy fuck, fuck," he says and although it might not be the sexiest terminology in the world, his lack of word choice turns me on. This is a man who makes money off writing thousands of words a day, and here I am, making him forget every single one of those words with just my mouth.

My hand pumps in rhythm with my mouth. If my lips go down, my hand goes up. Over and over, and the curse words falling from Simon's mouth are all the motivation I need to keep going even after my jaw starts to hurt, and I feel as if I'm going to get lockjaw from sucking so hard.

"If you don't stop now, I'm going to come all down your throat, Greer," he practically growls.

It only makes me work faster.

"Greer." He groans and then I feel the hotness of his orgasm slide down my throat. I swallow quickly, licking him clean before I sit up to find him watching me with wide eyes.

"What the fuck was that?" he asks.

I laugh. "Um, a blowjob?"

"Fucking hell, Greer."

I love how he says my name.

"Was that your first blow job?" Why else would he ask me that?

His deep laugh is addicting.

"Christ, no, but I sure as hell haven't ever had one that had me coming in less than five minutes. That was the world's best blow job."

I smile and lean back. "Too bad it's called a blow job. Talk about a mood killer with just a couple of words. I think the words sound ickier than the deed itself."

Simon crawls over me, capturing my mouth in a kiss.

Fun fact, kissing Simon is one of my new favorite things to do.

"Are you telling me that if I reached between your legs right now, you wouldn't be turned on by what you just said to me?"

I hold my finger up. "I did not say that."

He grins and then does exactly as he said, reaching between my legs.

"Jesus, I'd say that *really* turned you on."

"You have no idea," I say and grab him to kiss me again.

He settles between my legs, one hand reaching off the bed to my nightstand to grab a condom. We'd gone through the two in his wallet last night and had to break into the stash I have in my nightstand. Safe sex is never something to be messed with, and right now, I'm grateful that I always like to be prepared. I'm on the pill, but I have a feeling that wouldn't matter to Simon. After what he admitted to me yesterday, as much as I'd love to feel him bare, I won't put that stress on him.

He rolls it on and slips inside me.

It's like the first time all over again, and I have to remember to breathe, remind myself to come back down to earth.

He peppers kisses against my neck, trailing down to my chest. His hips move at a slow, deep pace. I reach behind him to wrap my hands against this firm butt, as if I'm helping him with his thrusts so that he can get deeper and deeper.

"Simon," I moan as he takes one of my nipples into his mouth, sucking on it for just a moment before letting it go with a pop and blowing on it. After he repeats that on the other side, I find myself shattering underneath him, happily ruined for any man who tries to come after him.

Simon's release arrives in the middle of mine, and together we chase the high of being together.

I want to live in this moment forever.

By lunch, I've officially had more orgasms in the last twenty-four hours than I have in my entire life.

I'm not complaining, but I am starving. The rumble in my stomach is a good sign.

In only Simon's oversized shirt from last night, I make my way to my kitchen.

I open the fridge, wondering what I'm going to make, when his arms come around my waist until I step back so that he can hug me.

"Simon, we need to eat."

"I know, but I just can't seem to get enough of you."

I spin to face him and let him kiss me. Then I push him back. I want him to stay with me all day, but I know he doesn't get much time alone, so I don't want him to feel obligated.

"Do you need to get home to get some work done?"

"Are you trying to get rid of me?"

"No." I start looking in the cabinets. Not much for food options there either. "I just assumed you might need to work."

He doesn't reply. I glance over my shoulder. His eyes are glued to my legs.

"Simon," I scold flirtatiously.

"Sorry." He sits at my kitchen island. "No. I don't need to write today. I was thinking I'd take the day off."

I face the cabinets again so he can't see the grin on my face. I'm smiling so big my cheeks hurt.

"That's nice."

"Mm-hmm, I thought maybe we'd order pizza, watch a movie, and then go get ice cream."

Just like I'd do with my mom. Like I told him yesterday. I swallow the lump in my throat and blink away any tears before I turn around.

"That sounds like a really good day."

"Yeah, it does."

A few moments pass as we just remain in my kitchen staring at each other. For heaven's sake, he just said let's order pizza, watch a movie, and get ice cream, but by the way he's looking at me, you'd think we just decided to move in together or get married.

I'm the one who chooses to move first. I open a drawer and pull out a to-go menu for Wind Valley's local pizza shop downtown. Simon sits up to lean over the island.

"Is that a drawer full of to-go menus?"

"Yes," I say and bump the drawer closed with my hip.

He chuckles. "And here I thought you were very strict with your diet."

I point at him with the menu. "You can still go out and eat healthy. You just need to know what your body is missing. Being healthy never has to mean missing out."

He holds his hands up in surrender.

Then he's off his chair and chasing me around the kitchen in a heartbeat. When he catches me, he props me up on the counter, spreads my legs, and reminds me who gets the last word.

For the record, it's him.

About a half hour later, we finally order pizza and pick out a movie.

* * *

"Let me have a bite of yours," Simon says, reaching over me with his spoon to steal some of my moose tracks ice cream.

I don't argue, I just do the same to his bubble gum.

I get one of the little pieces; it crunches in my mouth.

"You know, I feel like these were chewier when I was a kid. Now it's like I'm eating little frozen candies."

"I was thinking that too."

I get up to put the lid on mine, and he follows me.

I grab a sticky note off the counter and write "candy, not gum" with a little heart on his and then put it in the freezer.

He folds his arms and leans against the counter.

"Why do you do that?"

"Do what?"

"Put stickies on everything."

"Oh, um, my mom used to do it. Like, she'd put a sticky on my cereal boxes when she went to work early. So when I woke up and went to eat, I got a note from her even though she couldn't be there."

"Your mom sounds like a pretty great woman. I'm sorry I never met her."

I shrug. "We didn't really know each other then."

"Do you think she would have liked me?"

I glance up, meeting his gaze at his question.

She'd have loved him.

"I think so," I tell him.

He kisses my forehead and then points to the couch. "Another—"

His words are cut off by his cell phone ring.

He pulls it from his pocket, and we both look down to see his mom calling.

"Hey, Mom," he answers and moves into the living room while I wash our spoons and pizza plates and put them in the dishwasher.

"Oh, really? Okay, yeah. Five minutes, huh. Yeah, I'm home."

My heart immediately sinks.

He's going home.

I knew this is how the weekend would end, but I thought we'd have one more night.

"Okay, I'll see you in a few minutes."

I don't even try to pretend like I didn't hear every word when he steps back into the kitchen.

"I… Grey wanted to come home tonight so that he could work on some football stuff with me tomorrow since it's still the weekend."

"Okay. Of course."

"I—"

"It's fine. You don't have to say anything. We knew this was one weekend, and it was a great one."

He nods, and I have to look away because even though I knew, it doesn't make it hurt any less.

"Yeah, except, I don't want one weekend," he says quickly.

I glance up as he steps toward me.

"I don't know what this is, and I can't give it a name or give you some big commitment that you're looking for, but I know that one weekend with you isn't enough for me."

He's so honest about where he stands. It makes me want him even more than before. He isn't trying to trick me or lead me on, he just tells me the raw, honest truth.

And as much as I know I should say I can't do that because I want commitment, the words leave my mouth as if I have no control.

"It's not enough for me either."

He grins. "Good."

Then he grabs his things and backs up to the door.

"Leave your bedroom light on tonight, okay?"

"Okay."

He rushes to me for one more kiss and then jogs out the door.

I should know that I've just set myself up for failure, but all I can think about is this man who makes me feel not so alone anymore.

It's a nice feeling. Too nice, and one I'm not ready to let go.

CHAPTER TWENTY-FOUR
SIMON

By Sunday afternoon, I'm going crazy looking for a reason to be around Greer. I realize that whatever is happening between us will more than likely end up complicated, but she's this new light in my life.

Maybe somewhere along the way, if she's around enough, the part of my brain that keeps telling me I can't have a happily ever after will fade. You'd think it would be that easy to change my own fate, but it's not. I had the chance once, and it was taken from me. I won't go through that again.

I glance up just in time to see the football Grey tossed flying at my face. I barely catch it.

"Dad, pay attention," he says, as if he's the parent and not me.

"Sorry, bud."

He turns to Greer's house behind me.

"Why do you keep looking at Greer's house?" he asks, and I chuckle. I have to remind myself that this kid is eleven, and he's a lot smarter than I give him credit for.

I shrug and toss the ball back.

"I'm just distracted."

"By Greer," he says as more of a fact than a question as he catches the ball.

"By a lot of things."

He throws again, this one a lot harder than the last and resulting in a loud smack against my palms.

"Greer being one of them," he adds.

I tuck the ball under my arms.

"Why do you think that?"

He shrugs, and I swear I see myself more in him in this moment than ever before.

"I just… you look at her weird. But it's a good weird. It's why I told the team you were dating."

I nod slowly, not really sure how to reply.

"It's okay if you like her," he adds when I haven't said anything.

"Oh yeah?" I say, grabbing the ball to toss it back.

"Yeah. She's cool. And I like that she makes you happy."

I shake my head and neither of us says another word as we pass back and forth.

"You should invite her for dinner tonight," Grey says out of nowhere.

My heart instantly races at the thought of being near her.

"She cooks for us all the time. We should cook for her."

I chuckle at the fact that my own son has more ideas on how I can see Greer again than I do.

"Yeah, maybe we should."

"Good. Now that that's settled," he says with a nod, tossing the ball to the ground and resting his foot on it, "I need to talk to you about something."

For a moment, I get a glimpse into the future of me talking to a grown man.

"What's that?" I ask and nod toward the porch. He follows me, and we both sit, grabbing our individual waters and taking a drink. He leans forward, his elbow on his knees and his head drops between them.

Whatever is on his mind, he's clearly worked up over it.

I sit up a little straighter, ready for whatever he's about to say.

The suspense is killing me.

"I kissed a girl last weekend, and I think Greer will know what I need to do next."

I almost bark out a laugh, but then it hits me. Not the he kissed a girl part—we will definitely get to that—but the other part.

"Wait, you think Greer will have better advice than me?"

"Yes. She dates. You don't. She knows what girls like."

As much as that stings, he's right.

"I still know a little something."

"Oh yeah? Is that why you're just staring at her house and not doing anything about it?"

I reach over and ruffle his hair.

"Don't forget you're only ten."

He swats my hand away and stands.

"Eleven."

I laugh.

"My bad."

He grabs my phone off the patio table and tosses it into my lap.

"Call her."

Then he heads into the house, and I sit there in shock.

When the hell did my son become my own personal wingman?

* * *

The bread is burning, smoke coming from the oven, by the time Grey opens the front door to let Greer in.

I hear her and Grey talking but have no idea what they're saying as I try to wave the smoke away and hope that the alarms don't go off.

"Don't worry, Dad, Greer brought food too. We won't starve."

I cast a quick glare at my son before my eyes meet Greer's, who is smiling. The frustration I'm having with dinner fades. Everything about her being here tonight is different, and I can already feel the peace she's brought me in just the few seconds she's been in this room.

"I'm gonna go finish my game," Grey yells when he's already halfway down the hall headed for the stairs.

"Do you want help?" Greer asks, setting the dish in her arms down.

"Any chance that's a full meal?"

"Nope."

She rubs my back with one hand while the other lifts the towel I'd placed over the bread to hide it.

"Charred, my favorite," she teases.

I pinch her side and she yelps, but I kiss her before she can say something else snappy. The bread might be burned, but the spaghetti will be perfect. That's a hard dish to mess up.

Greer rises to her toes to kiss me back, and I wrap my arms around her to hold her.

"Are you sure it's okay that I'm here?" she asks quietly.

"Yes." I nod toward the stairs. "You know as well as I do that he has his headphones on and can't hear us."

"I know, but I feel like this would be a bad impression for him."

She's not wrong.

"He just thinks I have a crush on you."

"Ah," she says with a smirk.

"I also think he had ulterior motives to invite you here." I stir the sauce and lean into her. "He kissed a girl. My kid kissed a girl at this age. I don't even think that was on my mind back then."

Greer pats my shoulder.

"Don't read too much into it. He kissed her and ran away."

"What? How do you know that?" I put the lid back on the sauce.

"He just told me, and then he asked me what he should do next. I said he should ask you."

I nod. "Good. thanks."

"But flowers and an apology that he might have hurt her feelings is also a good place to start."

I let out my breath and lean in to kiss her.

"Thank you for that too."

Knowing Grey is hiding in his room, I press my lips to her once again, let the kiss linger.

What I wouldn't give to have a repeat of her kitchen yesterday. The thought of her on my table, open and bare to me, leaves my cock straining against my jeans.

I back up.

"Maybe we leave any more touching till after dinner."

"Oh, you think I'm staying that long, do you?"

"I hope you are. Plus, I have something I want to show you."

She moves to grab some plates and puts them on the table, moving around freely as if this is as much her home as it is mine.

Another thought crosses my mind.

What if she lived here with me?

I watch her set the table, letting the idea sink in.

Obviously, I'm not going to ask her. That would be insane. But the idea remains, mostly straying into what-ifs. The other part of it says it's too risky.

I focus on my breathing, hoping she won't pick up on my inner battle.

I don't know another single person in the world who looks at love the way I do. Something to be feared instead of welcomed.

Grey runs down the stairs, and if I didn't know better, I'd say it was a herd of elephants before he runs into the kitchen, sliding across the floor on his socks and picking his spot at the table.

Conversation comes easy between the three of us, and when the topic of planning our week arrives, I'm half tempted to tell Greer that I don't need her. It feels wrong to sleep with her and pay her to watch my kid.

But her words from the other day come back, and I know there is no way I can take this job from her.

After dinner, we pick out a movie, some new action movie

on Netflix. Grey falls asleep before the ending, so I carry him up to his room to put him to bed.

When I come back down, Greer is picking up the living room and folding the blankets we'd been using.

"You don't want to finish the movie?" I ask.

She smirks. "As if you were going to come back down here to watch it."

I take the blanket from her hands and toss it on the couch.

"You're right. I have other plans for you."

I grab her hand and lead her to the basement.

"Where are we going?"

"I told you I wanted to show you something," I say, leading her through the main room.

"Oh, your office? It's nice."

"Hold the excitement," I say and then grab the book that opens my secret library.

As soon as it begins to open, Greer's face lights up.

"Oh my gosh, Simon. Has this been here this entire time?"

"Yep. Grey knows about it and so does Calla, but I've never shown it to anyone else."

"No one?" she asks, spinning to take in the room. "It's so pretty. How many books are in here? It has to be a few hundred."

"Just about, yeah."

"Oh and look," she rushes to one of the shelves. "All of your books."

She grabs one off the shelf.

"This one has a library sex scene. A private library sex scene to be more specific. You didn't by any chance write it in hopes that one day that would be you in this room, did you?"

My chest swells with pride. "Exactly how many of my books have you read?"

"All of them," she flirts. Then she moves to the chair, her hands resting on the back of it as she bends over. "Is this how it starts?"

I groan and quickly close the secret door.

By the time I turn back around, Greer is unbuttoning her blouse and opening it to show me the lace bra that barely covers her breasts.

In two strides, I'm grabbing her face to kiss her.

"How quiet can you be?" I ask her.

"Pretty quiet if you keep my mouth busy."

"I can do that." I slip my tongue into her mouth.

We strip, never letting our lips part longer than it takes to remove our shirts.

"Bend over the chair like you were."

I take in her cheeky panties as she does it but know that I won't last much longer. It's been a whole day without being inside her, and my cock knows what it's missing. I loop a finger in the side of her panties and slide them down her legs. As soon as she steps out of them, I kneel behind her.

"Simon," she says on a breath as her eyes go wide watching me over her shoulder. "What are you doing?"

"Eating dessert," I say and do just that.

She presses herself back against my face and moans, so I lick faster; my fingers slide into her and play with her clit all at once.

"Oh god. Yes. Yesss!"

I need her to be a little quieter. I spin her quickly, stand, and cover her mouth with my own. I lift her to wrap her legs around my hips, and then I sit on the chair. I've lifted my ass to shrug my pants and boxers off when I realize I don't have my wallet.

"Fuck." I kiss down her neck. "My wallet is upstairs."

"Okay, go get it," she says in a hurried breath.

"I…"

God, I would love nothing more than to feel her with nothing between us. But this is new, and we aren't serious. She's already given me too much in the last forty-eight hours. I can't ask her for this too.

"I'm on the pill," she says quietly. "And I'm clean."

"Are you sure?" I ask. It's like she could read my mind. This woman is everything. She was made for me.

"Yes."

I finish removing my clothes, and she raises herself to help me. Once I'm naked, she sets herself back on my lap and slowly moves her hips back and forth.

"Greer, I'm a grown man, but if you keep doing that, I'm going to come right here before you've had a proper chance to ride me. So either you sit on my cock, or you move those hips faster and put me out of my misery."

She grins—she knew exactly what she was doing.

Reaching between us, she grips me in her hand, pumping up and down slowly two times before she lowers herself onto me.

She's so fucking tight.

I can never get enough of her.

She lowers a little before rising, only to repeat the process over and over, each time taking more of me. Finally, as if she can't handle it, she slams down on me. I know she wants to scream out, because instead of doing that, she kisses me, biting my lower lip.

Sweet sunshine Greer Harrison is a minx when it comes to sex, and I absolutely love it.

I meet her rhythm; our bodies moving in sync until I feel that familiar sting at the base of my spine.

"Baby, tell me you're close."

"Almost."

"Hold on to my shoulders," I say.

I need to get her there if I want her to come with me.

I pound into her from where I sit, our bodies slapping together and our breathing the only noise in the room. She lets out a soft moan, but by the way she now bites my shoulder, I know I'm giving her what she needs.

"Yes," she purrs into my ear. "Don't stop, Simon."

Faster and faster I pump, until she makes the smallest of squeaks in my ear, her breathing frantic.

I feel her pulse around me, and it's all it takes to trigger my own orgasm ripping through my body and spilling into hers.

I press soft kisses to her cheeks as we come down.

I still might not have any idea what we're doing, but I do know this.

Piece by piece, Greer is going to break this doubt in my mind. She can get me there.

I just hope I'm strong enough to hold on until she does.

CHAPTER TWENTY-FIVE
GREER

The next morning, I barely make it out my door before Simon is jogging off his porch to give me a good morning kiss.

It was unexpected, and it's the only thing I can think about as I push my bike into the studio and prop it against the wall by the window.

It's been a whole three days. I don't want my mind to run wild with whatever this thing between Simon and me could be. I can't forget what he told me in the car. He won't date. Not for real anyway.

Even knowing that, I can't remember the last time I had a smile plastered to my face 24/7 the way I have since Friday. It feels good to be wanted.

So, sooooo good.

I drop into my chair and spin.

I've missed this feeling.

"Well, well, well, look who finally showed up."

I flinch so badly; I almost fall out of my seat.

"Holy crap, Calla, what are you doing here?" I glance at my watch. "It's not even eight yet."

"I have an early morning, and I asked Willa to meet me here early. It helps that we finished in time for me to come see you."

She sips her coffee and sits in the chair across from me. Her eyes are laser focused on mine as she leans back.

"So, what's really going on between you and my brother?"

I knew this question would come. Simon is expecting it too. Although, I did have high hopes that she'd talk to him first so that I could be a little more prepared.

"Nothing."

Even as I say the word, I know there's nothing convincing about it.

"Nothing more than what you know, anyway."

She raises her left brow and smirks. Yeah, she doesn't buy it.

"Sure. Sure. So is that why he kissed you in front of me in our mom's kitchen?"

"He thinks you think we're dating, so it made sense."

"I called him out on it at the birthday party, and he didn't correct me. So he still kissed you even knowing that I know you aren't really dating."

There's no stopping the smile that appears on my lips.

"Really?"

"Yes, really. So tell me what's going on."

She seems irritated, and up until this moment, I didn't really think about how she would feel if we dated.

Shit, does this mean I'm so obsessed with meeting someone that I stopped thinking about how my choices would affect others? Am I a bad friend? How could I have not asked her about this before this moment?

Oh god, what happens if she tells me to stop whatever this is with Simon? It would make sense to call it now before I can let my thoughts get carried away, but being with Simon feels so freeing.

I'm not sure what I'd do.

"We're… are you mad? I'm sorry I never said anything. It all happened so fast."

She shakes her head.

"I'm not mad," she says with a big sigh. "More worried. I don't know. It's weird."

"Weird, how?"

"I haven't seen Simon show affection toward anyone the way he did with you since Grey's mom. I don't know. I don't want to make it weird talking about her. I'm not comparing you two, it's just—I don't know what to think of it."

My heart instantly warms. She loves Simon. It's clear. Not just from her words but how her eyes started to gloss over just now talking about him.

"You can talk about Grey's mom anytime you want, Calla. Simon knows he can too. She was their life, and now she's gone. I don't want anyone to ever think they need to avoid talking about her. Plus"— I pause and sigh myself— "Simon and I may not be really dating, but we are very attracted to each other. I'm not sure anything will come of it, but I'm enjoying my time with him while it's there."

She smiles softly and nods. "Just go easy on him, okay? If he messes up, it's because he's rusty as hell in the dating department."

I chuckle. She won't have to worry. I don't think a lot of people would understand this thing between Simon and me if I tried to explain it. Hell, I'm not sure I'd know how to explain it.

"All right, well, I love the guy, but if he messes up"—she points between us— "you and I can't change. You are a part of my life now. Let's keep it that way."

"Deal."

She stands with a nod.

"I better get this day started."

"Make it a good one."

"I will." She pauses at the door. "Hey, Greer?"

"Yeah?"

"Eww, you kissed my brother," she says, then laughs her way out the door.

My morning flies by. All my clients are on time, and no one cancels. I even had one sign on for another six months and then signed her sister up too. Keeping clients has never been a problem for me, but I'm still grateful each time they want to extend their one-on-one sessions.

I pack up the studio and pop over to say hi to Willa. With my schedule this summer, she and I haven't had as much time to catch up. But Calla and Beck's reception is this weekend, so I make a mental note to make extra time for her.

After all, I wouldn't have my dream job if she hadn't gone after hers.

I step over my bike and tighten my helmet before pushing off and heading toward Simon and Grey's.

Grey and I have ninja warrior camp today. I'm excited to go. It's only a few weeks before they have their first of three end-of-camp competitions. Which means summer is only five more weeks.

Since that's all the time that Simon and I agreed on for me to watch Grey, does that mean that we'll call it quits on whatever this is at that time too?

Five weeks of Simon and I'm just supposed to wave goodbye one day, go home, and pretend nothing ever happened between us.

No way in hell can I pull that off.

I pull up in front of their house, and Simon steps off the porch.

Well, this is new. First it was the Simon who scowled at me whenever I'd ride by, then it was the Simon who would stare me down as I walked up to his house each day, then it was the Simon who would close his computer to greet me when I arrived. Now it's the jog-down-the-steps-with-a-flirty-grin-to-meet-me-in-the-grass-for-a-kiss Simon.

You won't hear me complain about this. Not one bit.

He spins his hat backward right before snaking his hands around my lower back. I groan at his smooth movements right before he kisses me.

He holds me tight, and his tongue slips past my lips for a quick moment before he pulls back.

"How was your morning?"

"It was good. It went fast. What was your favorite scene to write this morning?"

He taps his chin.

"Would you judge me if I said it was along the lines of us last night in my library?"

I slap his shoulder and then hide my face.

"Please tell me you didn't write that."

"Oh no, I'd never write you and I in my books. But I do write sex, so it wasn't far off."

I shake my head with a smile and then move past him.

"Is Grey ready?"

"Just about. I was thinking of taking the afternoon off and coming with you."

I turn around and hold my hand up.

"You will do no such thing, Simon Stone. I'm here to help you. You can't just start taking afternoons off. My job here would become pointless."

He sighs. "I know, and I have a lot to get done."

"So get it done and you can hang out with us after."

"Yeah." He falls into step with me. "You're right."

"Plus, I have a good idea for dinner, and if you get all your work done, maybe I'll stay to eat it with you."

He pulls me into him. "Only if I get to have you for dessert."

Our lips are inches away when the door swings open and Grey zooms out with his ninja attire.

"Let's do this. Dad, you're gonna be so proud when you see me in a few weeks. I've gotten so good, it's not even funny."

Both Simon and I laugh.

"I said it's not funny," Grey repeats.

"I know, I'm sorry," Simon says with a hand over his mouth. Then he high-fives his son, who follows me to my house to get my car.

"See you both tonight!" he shouts.

I pull onto the road as soon Grey and I are both buckled, and he tells me about how he apologized to the girl he kissed and ditched. She said it was fine because she wasn't sure if they were supposed to keep going or what they would talk about afterward.

They're happily back to friends-only status right now. But no worries—if they change their minds, he'll come to me first.

Let's just keep that between me and Grey for now.

We head into the ninja studio, and Grey hustles into the classroom, hitting knuckles with some of his friends as they get ready.

"Hi, Greer."

I glance up to see his coach.

"Hi, how are you?" I stand to meet his gaze. It feels weird to hold a conversation when one of the two parties is sitting.

"I'm good. Listen, I know this is forward, but would you like to get dinner sometime?"

"Oh, I—" First Grey's football coach, who I'm positive wanted to ask me out at Grey's party, and now his ninja coach too. What am I supposed to say?

Greer from a few weeks ago would have jumped on this opportunity. Greer today is… even if I said yes, my heart wouldn't be there, and that's not fair to me or him.

"You can think about it. Maybe let me know when class is over."

He backs up with a smile and a wave. He's just about to enter the class when I say, "I'm sorry. I'm seeing someone right now."

"Oh." The smile on his lips drops for only a split second. "Makes sense. He's a lucky guy."

Then he taps the doorframe and begins class.

I reclaim my seat and process the last three minutes.

A single man, clearly ready for a relationship, just asked

me out, and I turned him down because I don't want to end whatever I have going on with a man who never wants to date.

Yep. That about sums it up.

I blow out a breath.

Hell, Greer, I sure hope you know what you're doing.

CHAPTER TWENTY-SIX
SIMON

This past week, my writing has been on fire. Not only have I hit my word count every single morning before Greer showed up to watch Grey, but I'm ahead. New versions of books have been uploaded to sites, film decks for possible movies have been created and sent to either my agent or publisher, and next year's synopsis for each book is ready for my editor to edit. Hell, I even have next month's newsletters ready to go.

To say the past week has been motivating is an understatement.

I grab a tie from my closet and step back into my room to put it on in front of my dresser, but Grey comes in.

"Do I have to wear a tie?" he asks, holding one up that is now in a knot around his neck.

I chuckle. "No."

He whips it over his head. "Good."

Then he flops onto my bed and watches me in the mirror. His eyes are focused on my hands as they adjust my tie.

"Do you want me to help you with yours?"

He nods and grabs the one he discarded a moment ago.

I leave my collar flipped up before kneeling to help him.

"Who taught you to do this?" he asks.

"My dad—well, more so my mom. Grandpa worked a lot, and so whenever I had something for school where I had to dress up, she'd help me."

He lets it sink in.

"Do you think Mom knew how to tie one?"

Although I did love his mother, our relationship was anything but typical. Everything happened so fast, and we never attended an event where we had to dress formally. So I have no idea if she knew how to tie a tie or not.

"She knew how to do a lot of things, but I'm not sure about that one."

"What was she the best at?"

"Singing," I answer without a second thought. "She loved singing, and she was good at it. She was even going to school for music when we met."

"She was?" His face lights up. "What kind of music did she sing?"

I finish his tie and then mine. I'm not opposed to him asking questions about his mom, but he doesn't do it often, so I'm a little thrown that he's doing it today.

"She loved country music."

He laughs. "You never listen to country music."

"It's not my favorite, but I listen to it every now and then."

"Do you think Greer listens to country music?"

With my hands on my hips, I spin to face him, completely flabbergasted at his line of questioning.

"You sure are full of questions today," I say, my eyes

snapping to the window as Greer walks through her room. She's not looking this way, but the emerald-green dress she has on makes my breath catch in my throat.

"I'm just curious." He jumps off my bed and runs out of the room.

Kids are weird.

I finish getting ready, and I'm just down the stairs when there's a knock at the door.

The front door hasn't even shut before I'm spinning Greer around, pushing her against the wall and pressing my lips to hers.

"Stay the night tonight," I say between kisses. I'd planned to ask her at the reception, but seeing her right now—well, now works.

She moans.

"You know I can't."

"You can. You just won't."

"What if Grey sees me?"

"Then he sees you."

I hear the bathroom faucet running upstairs, so I know Grey is busy and won't be down for a few more minutes.

I take advantage of our free time together and kiss Greer again. This time, I let the kiss linger, my tongue sliding over her cherry lips to mingle with hers. I love that her mouth always tastes like wintergreen. It's a sweet treat when I kiss her, and I'll never look at mints the same way again.

Her hands thread into my hair, tugging as what I planned to be a few sweet kisses to greet her turn into something more desperate. Kissing Greer is like nothing I've ever experienced. It's like the first time every time, and I can't get enough of her.

Feet race down the stairs, and she pushes me off her.

She's hanging her jacket on the hook behind the door by the time Grey makes it down the stairs.

"Greer!" Grey yells and then bombards her with a hug. "Do you know how to tie a tie?" he asks.

What's going on with this kid?

"I do. My mom taught me," Greer answers proudly.

"Oh."

I see the wheels turning in his mind, but before I can say anything, he says, "My dad is going to teach me."

Greer glances at my outfit, her gaze taking a slow perusal of me from head to toe. She winks.

"Well, it looks like he knows what he's doing, so you're in good hands."

Grey looks between us and smiles before running back to his room without a word.

"Is he okay?" she asks on a laugh.

"I think so. He was asking me about his mom a little bit ago."

I don't share that he also asked about her and the music. I'm not saying it means anything, but there is a chance Grey might be thinking about Greer in a motherly role.

Fuck. Is that a good thing?

"I need to check your fridge really fast for things I want to cook next week."

Greer heads for the kitchen, and I take a breath.

What will this do to Grey when Greer and I stop what we're doing? He knows it's not real, right? Maybe Greer is onto something when she said she can't stay and chance Grey seeing her.

But hell, I can't uninvite her now.

I don't want to, but I should.

She deserves better.

The thought creeps in like it always does, but this time, another one creeps in with it.

Grey deserves better.

I'm playing with a lot of emotions in my selfishness to have Greer.

And that alone means I should call this whole thing off, but right now, I'm not sure which scares me more: not taking a chance with her or watching her meet and spend her life with someone else.

* * *

It doesn't take long for Calla and Beck's reception to get into full swing. Considering they didn't have a ceremony and guests are just showing up simply to drink, eat, and dance, people are having a blast.

Grey especially. I'm not sure there's anyone here he hasn't cruised on by on the dance floor.

I think Greer has zero problems being out there with him too. Greer is good at a lot of things, but rhythm is not one of them.

It makes me like her even more.

Fuck. What am I going to do?

If we keep going and don't name this or set an end date, I'm just going to hurt her. End date or not, every outcome results in me losing her. But hell, I don't want to think of a life without her.

I swallow the lump in my throat. I can't fall in love with her and lose her.

I can't… I can't go through that again.

"So how are things going with Greer?" my sister asks, waving at a couple I don't know and taking a seat next to me. "Fake or not, you two are getting close pretty quickly."

"We're just having fun," I say and sip my beer. I smile when I see Greer and Grey doing some kind of robot move over by the drink table. Grey has a root beer bottle in his hand, and Greer leans forward like he's holding a mike. Robots who sing. Sure, why not?

"Just having fun?" Calla repeats.

"Yeah."

I glance at Calla before averting my gaze back to the robot duo. I don't need to continue looking at my sister to know that whatever I said has caused her to worry.

"You know Greer isn't just a let's-have-fun kind of girl, right?"

"She is this summer."

I'm not sure why I said that. It felt wrong coming out of my mouth, but maybe I just need to justify what this is. Give my brain something else to focus on.

"What do you call what you two are doing?"

"Fun, Calla."

"But you two—"

"Are enjoying each other's company without worrying too much about it," I finish for her. "We got this."

Except that I am worrying about it, and I'm not so sure I got this.

I want to have this.

I do.

Calla nods, but I can tell she has more to say.

"You don't have to worry about me or Greer, Calla. Now

go enjoy your reception. Your husband is waiting to take you on the dance floor."

She watches me for a moment longer.

"Please don't hurt her," she says, taking a step back.

"I won't."

My sister forces a smile. "Or at least you won't intend to."

She turns before I can say anything else.

Of course I don't intend to hurt Greer. That's the exact reason why she deserves better. She deserves a man who isn't scared to take a chance on love. Whose fear of losing someone again doesn't take over every single happy thought. A man who can give her everything she wants in life. A man who doesn't have to fake date her as an excuse to touch her.

Fuck.

I have to let her go.

I glance up to see her watching me as Grey attempts to do the moonwalk in front of her. She waves for me to join them, and despite all my thoughts just now, I get up and do the slide until I reach them. Grey hoots and the rest of the guys who are on the dance floor cheer.

If tonight is the last night with Greer before I let her go, I want it to be one to remember.

CHAPTER TWENTY-SEVEN
GREER

I wish I could tell you exactly when in the evening that I decided tonight was the night Simon and I needed to talk, but I can't. I just know I went to Calla and Beck's reception to have fun, and now I'm riding in the passenger side of Simon's truck worrying about what I'm going to say to him. Or how I'm going to say it.

Maybe it was when he held me on the dance floor or the kisses he snuck when no one was looking, or maybe it was the way his hand never left mine. But something clicked in my brain and this right here, nights like this, are exactly what I want. No other man is going to make me feel this way. Ever. I know it.

There has been something forming between Simon and me this entire summer, and this last week only confirmed what I refused to accept. Simon is the guy I want. He's the man I need.

He's never been one to date, and I know why. But this thing between us—it feels real. I can't be alone in that feeling.

Heck, this is how effortless being in a relationship should be, right? I'm starting to think I was given a long list of horrible dates to bring me to this moment. Because Simon and I need each other. We can help each other.

It has to be us.

"All right, you haven't spoken a word since we left. What's going on in that head of yours?" Simon says quietly as he pulls onto our street.

I glanced at the back seat where Grey fell asleep almost instantly after he got in.

I smile. "He looks about five years younger when he sleeps."

Simons doesn't say anything, but he's watching me watch his son.

I sigh as he reaches over to lace his hand with mine while the other controls the wheel.

"Are you going to tell me or leave me hanging all night wondering what I can do to help?"

"Let's get Grey to bed, and then we can talk," I tell him.

He takes a breath as he pulls into his driveway. He gets out of the truck as soon as he's in park, walking around the front to open my door and then Grey's door.

"Hey, buddy, let's get in the house, okay?"

Grey grumbles something but gets out and shuffles his way inside, with Simon and me behind him. Simon slides his hand over my lower back to pull me close and kisses the top of my head.

I'll tell you what, if he doesn't feel the same, no man, and I mean no man, can kiss my head ever again. It won't be the same. It won't hold the same feeling of comfort and safety the way it does when Simon does it. It's so natural to him.

I don't want to miss this.

"Wait here," Simon says just before he follows Grey up the steps.

Something about the way he said those two words make me pause. He didn't say, *go to my room and wait for me,* or *make yourself at home, I'll be right back.* He said *wait here,* as if he wants me to stand in the doorway. As if he's going to come back down and say goodnight before sending me on my way.

I'm not sure where to look, so I fidget in place, not even bothering to take off my coat.

How did so much between us change with two words?

I blow out a breath.

You know what? I'm probably just overthinking every detail on account of what I'm waiting to talk to him about. Allowing my mind to play out all the worst-case scenarios so that when he does say he, too, wants this to be real, it'll be the best.

A few more minutes pass.

A week is too soon for me to ask him this, right?

Almost a decade's worth of thoughts can't be altered in a week, can they?

Before my thoughts can run too wild, Simon appears and points to the door.

"I'll walk you home."

Damn. Talk about being dismissed.

Something happened tonight. He's shutting down.

We walk side by side, and I'm very aware of his woodsy cologne. I'm also very aware of the fact he isn't touching me.

"I had fun tonight," I say as we reach my door.

He slowly backs up, his head dropping on a sigh.

"I think we need to stop what we're doing here," he says in almost a whisper. He can't even look up.

I gently touch his chin and force him to look at me.

"Did something happen tonight?" I ask.

He shakes his head.

"Okay." I take a deep breath. I could tell him everything—how I think we should be more, that we can be more. But something has him spooked. "Should we sleep on it and talk more tomorrow? It's almost one, and I'm beat."

I squeeze his hand reassuringly.

"Greer, there won't be more to talk about tomorrow. I'll see you on Monday."

He says his goodbye, but he doesn't move. In fact, he steps closer, one hand reaching for me before he pulls it back.

"We can slow down," I suggest.

I hear him loud and clear, okay? But maybe this is why he feels like he can't have it all. No one ever stuck around to fight for him when his mind starts to think the worst. I know I can't change his mind tonight, maybe not even tomorrow or next week, but I can wait. He's worth it.

"No, that— Greer, this whole thing… I can't lose you."

"So you're going to push me away instead. Isn't that the same thing?"

"No."

"Yes."

"If we stop now, any feelings that may be here will fade faster and easier."

"Maybe. Maybe not."

"Greer, stop arguing with me," he says on an almost laugh. "I'm trying to end this thing."

"I know." I cross my arms. "You're doing a shit job too."

"Greer," he groans. "You're so—"

"Stubborn? I know." I step off my porch toward him and cup his cheek before pressing to my toes to kiss him. He lets me too.

When I drop back to my heels, he says, "You deserve better than me."

"Let me make that choice on my own."

"I'm trying to protect you."

"No, you're running before *you* get hurt."

"Damn it, Greer. I'm trying to do the right thing here."

"Well, stop. You don't get to decide this one on your own."

Instead of replying, he steps back.

"I'm sorry, Greer. I really am. I just can't do this."

He needs to turn and walk away. He needs to put space between us, but he doesn't. It's like he's waiting for me to keep arguing with him. Like if we stand here just a little longer, one of us will do or say something that might change his mind.

As much as I would love to be that someone for him, the only person who can do that is himself.

"All right," I say and step back. "Just know that I'll be right here, waiting, when you can."

Some people might think I'm crazy or a silly woman to wait for a man, but they're wrong. If it's the right man, he'll be worth the wait.

If I've learned anything this summer, it's that you can't rush falling in love.

CHAPTER TWENTY-EIGHT
SIMON

I did the right thing.

I did.

I lean back in my chair and glance at the clock. It's time for me to call it a day and go upstairs, but just like the last three days, my heart sinks at this moment.

The one where I reach the top step and hear the happy chatter of my son and Greer from the kitchen. They'll both laugh, and I'll pause, soaking up her laugh before I step into their space and ruin the moment.

The worst part? You'd almost never know that something happened between us. Greer still continues to smile at me when she sees me, she talks to me as if we're still longtime friends. I want both of those things from her, but she does it so well. Maybe too well. Still, sometimes when I catch her gaze on me longer than it should be, I see the pain in her eyes. Or the desire. Because hell, it never escaped me.

I want to be with Greer more than ever now that I can't have her.

I take a breath, save my work, and head to the stairs.

I was supposed to have a new synopsis sent to my agent before the end of today, and it didn't happen. I'd moved the deadline up last week when I was on the high of life.

Now, the spark is gone.

I'm not an idiot. I know why, but it still sucks.

It's unusually quiet when I reach the top step, so I head straight for the kitchen.

There's no sight of Greer or Grey. I backtrack toward the living room, and that's where I spot them. Both asleep on the couch with the Hulu home screen on the TV. I take a quick look at my watch to see that it's just after eight. Yeah, I guess I did work later than normal tonight, but it's not crazy late.

Then again, Greer wakes up early to work and then comes here, and Grey has a full afternoon. After football camp she had a ninja warrior meeting for the end-of-the-year competition thing he has. Then he had a friend over, and I'm sure Greer played football with them.

I let out a half laugh.

Football, soccer, ninja warrior camp, playdates with kids, cooking and cleaning—after doing all those things for me, she still likes me for me and wants to be with me. She wants to wait for me, and I'm… scared as hell that it won't work out.

Am I overthinking this? Can it really be that easy to fall in love again?

I cross my arms and lean against the wall, watching the two of them. To say seeing her with my kid right now doesn't do something to me would be a lie. Greer is going to be in my life forever no matter what. Can I handle her being in it if we aren't together?

Fuck.

Things are so complicated. This is stupid.

I should just tell her that I'm an idiot, and I want to be with her. That we should give this a chance.

She stirs and wakes up, spotting me instantly.

"Simon," she says with a smile. "Why are you just standing there?"

"I was debating waking you up."

She looks at the clock. "Well, you definitely should have. I don't want to go to bed this early." She sits up, doing her best to not disturb Grey. "This guy, however, I bet he and Bill ran five miles playing in the yard this afternoon." She chuckles quietly. "Also, who starts calling their kid Bill at eleven?"

I laugh along with her.

"It throws me for a loop too. Every time Grey mentions him, I think he's talking about someone's dad."

Greer gets up, then straightens her clothes. "I'll get out of your hair."

When she moves for the door, the urge to follow her and tell her everything that just went through my mind hits me, but I stop.

I don't want to lose her, but committing before I'm ready, really ready, all because I'm afraid she won't be there when that time comes is foolish. It could cause more harm than good.

"Greer," I say, moving to get the door for her while she grabs a sweater and her purse.

"Yeah?" She turns; the scent of her body lotion surrounds me and my heart races. I miss having her this close.

My gaze falls to her bottom lip which she bites before snapping to her eyes.

"Thank you for everything you've done this summer."

Yeah, it's official. I'm an idiot.

The expression on her face stays the same as she just stares at me. If she was hoping I was going to say anything else, she doesn't show it.

"Of course. It's what you hired me for."

She turns for the door.

"Wait."

Fuck.

Just let her go.

"Yeah?"

There it is. The hope in her eyes.

I swallow, my hand reaching up to brush her cheek. Her eyes close as she inhales, her head tilting into my hand.

I know what I want. Why can't I just let myself have it? What do I have to do to convince myself that I can have it?

"Can I walk you home?"

"That's probably not a good idea, Simon."

I drop my forehead to hers.

"No, it's probably not."

I just want to stay here, with her this close to me.

She moves out of my hold quickly and is out the door before I can say anything else.

I stand in the doorway, watching her until she's safely inside her house, and then I retreat into mine.

If I'm going to be the man Greer deserves, where do I start?

I blow out a breath, carry Grey to his room, mentally prepare myself for him to wake up at the ass crack of dawn, and then I head down to my office and pull out a pen.

You can't fix yourself.

Yes, I can. I can and I will.

First things first. Turn every negative thought into a positive one.

Second thing, talk to someone. Share the thoughts I never share with anyone else and find a way to work through them.

I don't think it matters who it is as long as I'm talking.

I have to.

If I don't, this fear of losing Greer will take on a whole new meaning.

CHAPTER TWENTY-NINE
GREER

I've never been to a ninja competition before. I've caught a glimpse here and there of Grey in class, but still, I'm a first-timer, and the course set up looks pretty intense.

The gymnasium is half full when I get there, and although I could pick a seat up front, I opt for one in the back.

I didn't question whether or not I should come today. It's a Saturday, after all, and I'm not required to be here, but Grey is pretty excited about how far he's come this summer, so I wasn't going to miss it.

However, the last couple of weeks with Simon have been harder than I imagined they would be. He may have called it quits, but that heat between us, the one that draws us to the other anytime we are near, hasn't faded.

I just wish there was a way for me to help him realize all that he could have. That this distance between us can be changed all by one choice. His choice.

He can choose to be happy, but he won't.

Won't or can't?

"Hey!" Calla says, coming up the bleachers. "Why are you sitting up here?"

She plops down next to me with a small bag of popcorn and offers it to me.

I grab a small handful.

"I'm not sure your brother knows I'm coming, and I figured it was better if I stayed out of sight."

"Oh, he knows. Grey told him on the way here. I called him and heard it through the speaker. No one expected you to miss it. You and Grey are best friends now. No matter how stupid my brother is when it comes to relationships, he's stuck with you."

I know she's trying to be supportive, but I don't want him to be stuck with me. I want him to pick me. The way I pick him.

It was a long stretch to hope for it, and I know that by continuing on the way I am, there's a chance he will never change his mind.

It's one of those moments when you know you know, and I just need to be patient.

But I'll tell you what. Being patient isn't easy.

"Speaking of," Calla goes on, "has he said more to you about the two of you?"

My friends know me well, so it didn't take long for Willa to notice my mood change and for her to call Calla, who called a girl's night out. I told them everything. Even when Calla didn't want details on her brother, she listened. In the end, they both agreed with me that what Simon and I have doesn't come around often. It helped that he's Calla's brother, because even though she thinks he's a total moron, she gave me an extra-long hug for not giving up on him.

But how long do I wait? How long do I give him until I realize that he gave up on us for good?

"No, he hasn't said anything more."

"Damn."

"Yeah. Do you think I'm crazy?"

She laughs. "You're talking to a woman who married a guy she despises in Vegas all because they had one amazingly fun night together, and then who proceeded to drive him crazy so that he'd divorce her *and now* just celebrated her wedding reception. So no, I don't. Love does crazy things to people."

"Oh, I'm not sure we're in love."

"But aren't you? You're waiting for him, right? Isn't that love?"

"If it were, wouldn't he put me out of my misery?"

"Maybe he's waiting for the right time."

"Maybe."

"Look, it's not my place to say anything, but he's... making some changes, and I don't think he's doing it for just him. I think he wants to be with you too."

My eyes start to fill with tears.

"Waiting sucks," I say with a whisper.

She hugs me. "But it'll be worth it."

As soon as she says the words, I look up and spot Simon instantly. He's watching me from the gym entrance. It's as if the moment we're in the same room, we have to find each other.

He waves with a smile, Beck and Tobias following in after him while Grey races over to where his coach is sitting with the other kids in his class.

I wave back, hoping he can't see my glossy eyes.

I think I'm in the clear when he sits on a front bench next to some of the parents I've seen at practice.

"You can go sit with them if you want," I tell Calla.

She huffs. "And listen to the way Beck cheers Grey on? No thanks. I love that man, but he can be obnoxiously loud."

She loops her arm through mine as we watch our very first ninja competition. By the time the event is over for the night, Grey is in the top three. I couldn't be more proud of him and wish that I could be there to celebrate with him tonight.

I stall leaving for the sole fact that running into Simon on my way out is very possible.

I know it sounds silly that I'm avoiding him. I said I'd wait, but I don't want to smother him.

I want him to have the time and space he needs.

When I scan the open space and see no sight of Simon, I make my way down the bleachers.

I'm just off the last step when Grey calls my name.

"Greer! I knew you'd be here," he says and crashes into me with a hug. "Did you see me?"

"I did."

Despite his father standing behind him watching me with a heated gaze and making a hundred questions race through my mind, I smile at Grey. "I'm pretty sure you have more upper body strength than I do. You were pulling some pretty awesome stunt moves today."

"Thanks! Oh, here it is," he says and reaches behind me to grab a shoe that was under the first row. "Got it. Do you want to come get some food with us? Can she, Dad?"

I don't have to be looking at Grey to know he's got a hopeful look on his face as he looks at his father.

Simon takes a big breath and claps his hands. "I'm sure she has plans."

"Do you have plans?" Grey asks.

I glance at Simon, who shrugs.

"You're welcome to join us of course. You always are."

My heart is screaming for me to say yes, but even though that pull between us is there, my brain convinces me to do the right thing. Give him space.

"Can I take a rain check?"

Grey nods. "Okay. Thanks again for coming."

"I wouldn't miss it."

"Will you still come watch me for the next two weeks?"

"Of course."

"Cool."

He gives me one more hug and then starts for the door where a few of his friends are goofing around.

"So we'll see you on Monday?" Simon asks, and I nod.

"Yes. Monday."

"Have a good night, Greer."

"Have a good night, Simon."

He follows his son, then stops and turns.

"Greer?"

I look up.

"How about next week, you sit with me?"

I pinch my lips together to keep from smiling like a fool, but I nod.

"Okay."

"Okay," he repeats, smirking as he heads for the door, glancing over his shoulder once before they leave.

I blow out a breath and count to ten before I do the same.

It was something small, but the hope that was beginning to fade shines a little brighter now.

CHAPTER THIRTY

SIMON

The echo of chatter and kids shouting and practicing on the mats inside the gym are all I hear when we step into the gymnasium the next week.

It's week two of ninja warrior competitions for Grey, and I have a feeling he'll be at the top of the charts by the time the night is through.

I scan the gym as soon as we are inside.

"Are you really still not talking to Greer?"

"Greer and I talk," I say to Tobias as we wait for the competition to begin.

"You know what I mean."

I sigh and nod. "Yeah, I do. I will. Soon."

Since that night I found Greer and Grey asleep on the couch, I've worked hard to correct any negative thoughts about my future. But hell, I've been thinking about them for a long time, and it's hard to convince myself otherwise. I've googled and researched how to self-heal until my eyes burn from the screen. Plus, the guys and I had an hour-long chat one night and since then, they all text me each day to check in. Talking about it helps. It's nice to get different points of view on it. Especially from my friends who have had to fight their own demons to get to where they are in their relationships today.

I feel like I'm in a good place to talk to Greer, but just walking up to her and saying "Okay, I'm ready. I changed my mind" feels… lame and wrong.

It's why last week I invited her to sit with me today. I knew I'd see her all week, but I didn't want her to think that she needed to avoid me outside of that. And let me tell you, another week of not having Greer the way I want was pure hell.

It also solidified a lot for me. I write romance novels, for crying out loud. This isn't the time to slack off. This is grand gesture time. And that thought alone is huge progress for me.

"I'll talk to her soon."

"How soon?" he asks. "Because I'm pretty sure that Grey's football coach is talking to her right now, and his body language says that he knows she's single."

I follow his gaze, and anger flashes through me. Of course, he jumped. What the hell is he doing here anyway? This isn't football.

Shit. Did I take too long? Is he asking her out? Is she going to say yes?

She looks up.

"Well, she's not even looking at him, so I think I'm good."

"She can't wait forever."

"I know."

"So what are you waiting for?"

"The right time."

Tobias lets out a groan.

"What?" I ask.

"Don't be that guy. Don't be the guy who keeps waiting. Be the guy who goes after what he wants and takes it."

"I am."

"No, you're waiting for something bad to happen just so you can say *told you so*. Face it, Simon, nothing bad is going to happen. It's your turn, man. You need to go get your girl."

For as many times that I've talked to the guy in the past couple of weeks, that's the first time someone has made that comment.

Is that what I'm doing? Waiting around for something bad to happen?

What happens if it never happens? Then I've been making Greer wait for what? Nothing. To cause us both more heartache.

We take our seats in the front row again, and when Grey's turn comes up, all eyes fall on us the moment Beck starts yelling.

Greer is sitting with Calla in the same spot as last weekend. Her eyes flash to mine. I wave. She waves back.

Why isn't she sitting with me? I asked her to. She nodded like that was something she wanted. Fuck. Am I too late?

Tobias nudges me and then glares at me. "Man up."

I would laugh at his words, but hell, he's right.

As soon as the night's competition is over, Grey is sitting at number one. One more weekend and he'll be the winner.

He runs up to me with a giant smile.

"How cool was that?" he asks me.

I give him knuckles, and then he runs right by me to see Greer. I walk over, listening to their excitement over the night.

When they're finished, she looks up at me.

"You better watch out for this one," she says. "He's too good."

"Tell me about it."

She nods and then points over her shoulder.

"Well, I'll see you guys later."

"Bye, Greer!" Grey says as she leaves.

After a moment, Grey steps in front of me with raised brows.

"Dad?"

"Yeah?"

"If you like Greer, what are you waiting for?"

Did Tobias tell him to say that?

"You know what, bud? I don't think I am anymore." I put my hands on his shoulders and give him a squeeze. "Do you want to celebrate with ice cream and dinner or by us beating Greer home so we can win her back?"

"Umm, is that even a question? Win Greer back!" He heads for the door. He turns quickly to walk backward. "Then we get dinner and ice cream."

I chuckle at his response.

Sounds like a plan to me.

CHAPTER THIRTY-ONE
GREER

As soon as I get home, I change into sweats and slip on one of Simon's shirts that he left here. I'd sit and smell it like a real lovesick puppy, but I washed it, and the smell is gone.

Doesn't mean I won't wallow any less.

I was sure that by the end of the summer Simon would… it doesn't matter. I was wrong. I drag my feet down my hall and into the kitchen and grab the pint of ice cream I hide in the back. My Ben and Jerry's Cherry Garcia.

I snap a picture of it and send it in a group text with Willa and Calla.

WILLA

Shit.

CALLA

Oh, no. The full sugar version.

WILLA

What happened? I'm headed over.

CALLA

Me too.

I flop onto my couch and turn on the TV, scrolling through my phone to order a pizza online.

I'm going full-blown bum. I'm going to eat my feelings into next month, and I won't feel guilty about it for one minute.

An email notification drops down from the top of my screen. It's from one of the many stupid dating apps that I'm subscribed to. I'd deleted the apps, but not my accounts. So, I redownload the app, log in, and delete my account.

Then I log into the next one and delete that one too.

Once all three are deleted, I toss my phone to the side.

I feel like I did nothing but backtrack this summer.

I hate it.

I mean, technically, I'm just where I started. Alone.

Maybe I need to get another part-time job. My goal for the summer was to have a distraction, and I did. A big one too. One so big that my fear of never meeting "the one" is gone and a new fear unlocked. I'll never meet someone like him.

Last weekend, I thought maybe I stood a chance, then he never said a word this week, and tonight, when Calla begged me to sit in the back again so she didn't have to sit next to her screaming husband, I thought maybe that Simon would remind me to sit with him. It would be this cute moment when he asked me again, and I would say yes, and then somewhere in the night he'd hold my hand, and we'd slowly drift back to us.

But that didn't happen.

At the end of the night, he just said *bye*. Not to mention, the last time he saw me talking to Walker Blue, he jumped at the chance to claim me. Tonight, my attention to another man didn't even faze him.

My hope got the best of me.

My doorbell rings. I groan and once again drag my feet there. I swing it open in a dramatic fashion, assuming it's Calla or Willa on the other side.

But there isn't anyone there.

"What the hell?" I whisper. I poke my head out and look around. Nothing.

Figures. I'm trying to soothe a broken heart, and someone decided my house was the perfect place for ding dong ditch.

But just as I'm closing the door, a blue sticky note on the door catches my eye.

Please come next door in thirty minutes. —Simon

I read it over and over, my heart racing faster each time. I stand there long enough for Calla and Willa to both arrive and join me at the door.

"What are we looking at?" Calla asks.

I hold the note up.

She takes it and grins.

"How long ago did he leave this? And why is it on a sticky note? Why not just text you?"

"I don't know how long I've been standing here."

I don't answer her sticky note comment because my mind is running wild with what this means. He knows what sticky notes mean to me. Is that why he left one? To show me that even though he hasn't been here, he's been thinking of me?

I spin back around and race up to my room.

Calla and Willa are right behind me.

"I take it we're getting out of the sweats."

"We're getting out of the sweats," I repeat and flip through shirt after shirt and dress after dress until I find the right one.

I don't even know what I'm going over there for, but I know he wouldn't have left the note if it weren't for something big.

The doorbell rings again.

The girls and I all make eye contact in the mirror on my dresser as I'm putting my shoes on.

"I'll go get it," Willa says and runs downstairs.

I nod, moving to the bathroom to fix my hair.

Calla comes in with a huge smile.

"What do you know?"

She laughs. "Nothing, but if I did, I wouldn't tell you."

I smile, let out a nervous giggle.

"What if it's not what I think?"

She gives me a don't be stupid look in the mirror, and I nod.

"Maybe he just wants to talk."

"Well, it's still better than nothing."

"You're right."

"It's another sticky! It's another sticky!" Willa comes running into my room.

I grab it from her, and they both huddle behind me.

The front door is unlocked. Follow the notes. —Simon

"Oh my god. How cute is this!" Calla says and shoves me. "Hurry up."

I add a little mascara and lip gloss and then head out the front door, crossing our yards to his porch.

The next sticky has an arrow that points to his writing spot. His favorite table has the next one. Well, two.

The first time I saw you ride your bike past my house to meet the Realtor, I knew my life was about to change. I just didn't know how much. Go inside.

I push open the front door and find the next sticky where I usually hang my purse and coat if I have one.

Not seeing your things here feels wrong, like a part of me is missing.

I take a breath and hold the sticky to my heart.

I hear a noise from the backyard, but when I reach the kitchen, I find another sticky note on one of the kitchen table chairs.

This should be your forever spot with me and Grey.

Tears start to sting my eyes, but before they have time to fall, soft music plays outside. I step through the back door, where there are candles lit and white lights hanging over the patio. The sun is still setting, so they don't shine very brightly, but the entire ambiance screams something life-changing is about to happen and my heart is about to burst, waiting to see what Simon is going to do next.

"Greer," he says behind me. I spin to his voice. He's standing in the middle of the patio, hands tucked into his pants as he watches me. "I wasn't sure you were going to come."

"I lost a little track of time."

He nods, a smirk touching his lips.

"That makes two of us."

He reaches for my hand, then pulls me to him. When I'm close enough, he rests his forehead on mine.

"I'm sorry that I wasn't ready when you were. I'm sorry you had to wait for me. I'm sorry that for even a single second, I let you believe that being with you wasn't something I could do."

He says the words without a crack in his voice, but with each word, more tears threaten to fall, and my heart aches for him.

"I'm not perfect. I can't promise to be perfect. I still have a ways to go, and there are still a lot of things I don't know, but I do know this: all it took was one summer for me to fall in love with you, and I'd rather spend every waking moment of my life worrying about losing you than live one more minute without you."

And the tears break free. He swipes them away with his thumb.

"And I hate making you cry."

"These are happy tears," I say in a choked breath. "I promise."

With his hand under my chin, he guides my gaze to his.

"So I didn't take too long to come around?"

"A little," I say, and we both laugh. "But I'm still here."

I can't wait anymore. I crash my lips to his, then wrap my arms around him and hold him tight.

"Yes!" Grey shouts from his bedroom window, causing us to break the kiss and erupt into laughter again. "Hi, Greer!"

"Hi, Grey," I beam up at him.

He waves for a moment and then disappears. I take advantage of that moment to kiss Simon again.

"I missed you," I whisper between kisses.

"I love you," he replies.

"I love you too."

Suddenly, Grey is crashing out the back door, followed by Willa and Calla.

"Where did they come from?" Simon asks with a laugh.

"Oh my god, that was the cutest thing!" Calla gushes. She and Willa are both talking a mile a minute, and Grey joins them, quickly telling which parts were his idea and how he helped Simon.

"You're sure you're ready for this?" Simon asks, nodding to the trio on the patio.

"Yes," I say with confidence.

He pulls me in for another kiss as soon as Grey pulls the girls inside so he can show them his list of other ideas. We stay like this, slowly swaying to the music until the sun sets and the lights are shining over us.

Most people say that when it's real love, it should come easy and be simple. I don't think those people are necessarily wrong, but no two love stories are the same. Some people meet the right person at the right time, and some take a little more fight and patience than others. In the end, if it's real to you, you just have to make the right choice. For me, waiting for Simon was more than right.

EPILOGUE
TOBIAS

My entire life revolves around love.

Romance.

Intimacy.

Relationships.

Trust.

There's so much that goes into that one four letter word. More than me, a romance writer, will ever know. To every single person in the world, love is not defined the same. To be loved varies from person to person and over the last few years, I've watched it form five different times. Five different amazing and beautiful times.

I sit back in my chair, watching my friends in front of me.

The guys and I had been having a writer's session tonight. A much-needed couple of hours for all of us to get some work done. Yet, one by one, girlfriends, fiancés, wives, and kids have arrived to bring those friends home.

Me? I'll hang out here for another hour or so to check more off my to-do list.

I'm the only single friend in our group.

Solo.

Uno.

Me.

I'd like to say my time will come or that after watching my best friends find the love of their lives, I hope I'm next, but that's not me.

My moment has passed.

I've learned the hard way that no matter how hard you try, life won't always give you what you want. That the days are easier if you just go with the flow.

"Good night, Tobias," Simon calls out from the front entrance of The Space. He's got his arm wrapped around Greer's shoulders who's ruffling Simon's eleven-year-old son's hair. Last week he finally did the one thing we all thought he'd never do. He told Greer he loved her and let me tell you, the way he's changed in just the last seven days is mind-blowing. It's like this ten-ton weight that he'd been carrying around has vanished and for the first time in over a decade, he's actually living.

His life right now has all the elements for a love story and the happiness I feel for him is why I love what I write.

"You kids stay out of trouble," I reply and hold my hand up to wave goodbye.

They all return the gesture and head out the door.

I watch them walk down the street for a beat before I decide to open the email my agent, Doug, sent me earlier today. I hate talking about myself, so when I saw the email pop up with a questionnaire, I ignored it in a heartbeat.

When you get picked to be the author of the month in the

romance world's most beloved magazine, it's expected they want to know more about you.

I let out a sigh and open the attached document.

The first few questions are typical. Name, pen name, how many books I have, what genre I write, and so on.

But it's about halfway down that a question I've never seen before makes me sit back with a smile as I read the line out loud to no one.

"Of all your friends and family who know you write in the genre you write, when you finally told them, is there one moment that stands out the most to you?"

Hell, yeah there is.

I don't even have to think about the answer to this one. It was just a little over twelve years ago and it's my favorite memory from my college years.

I let out a chuckle and shake my head.

It's a night I'll never forget.

It's a night that changed my life forever.

"Happy birthday to one of the best guys I know, Tobias, and congratulations on your first book deal, Zane!" Beck cheers loudly before he, Zane, Simon, Hero, Graham, and I clink our shot glasses together.

The Fireball burns all the way down.

One by one, they slap me on the shoulder and fist bump Zane before wandering back into the living room where the majority of the party is taking place.

About a year ago, the six of us met in a creative writing class, where we discovered we're all male romance writers. I don't have to explain how that small fact brought us together. We've been a tight group from day one. I've had friends in the past who were supportive of my dream to write books, but nothing compares to having best friends who share the same goals as you. They just get it.

About a month ago, I rented an off-campus house. Beck, Simon, and Hero live here with me. Graham and Zane have their own apartment.

But tonight is the first party I've had here. It's June. It's my birthday month, and tonight has been so great that I'm considering making this a tradition. Not just for my birthday, but because during the school year, the guys and I have such busy schedules that somehow, we manage to cram in writing time with, but to actually hang out, have some beers, and enjoy ourselves, those are rare times.

Like I said, we all have big goals. Bestsellers, six-figure contracts, movie deals, serial show deals, audio deals, billboard signs, and so much more.

Determination and dedication aren't something we lack.

I lean in the doorway between the kitchen and the living room. I don't know half the people here. The turnout looks like word spread. Living in a college town can do that. But I don't mind it.

I'm glad I could host a fun night like this for everyone.

"Dude, look," Hero says, coming up behind me as he cracks open a new beer. "Who is that?"

He nods to the front door where a group of girls just walked in.

"Which one?" I ask, my gaze instantly falling on the last one. She's taller than the others, but not by much. Maybe five-ten, five-eleven. She's got on a pair of cut-off shorts, slip-on sneakers, and a pink one-shoulder top that really brings out the color of her tan skin. She has straight, shiny brown hair pulled into a high ponytail. It's so dark that it might actually

be black. I'd need to get closer to know. Her big brown doe eyes scan the room as she takes a breath. My guess is, she doesn't know anyone here. I should be a good host and introduce myself while offering her and her friends a drink.

"The one in the blue dress," Hero says.

I smile.

I have no clue who either of them is. I'm just glad he wasn't checking out the same woman as me.

"No clue. But this is our house, so let's go over there."

Hero is one step ahead of me, then I hear a crash in the kitchen behind me. Some guy just dropped a whole tray of shot glasses. I sigh, letting my buddy take over greeting our new guests.

"This is why we set out the paper cups," I say and point to the stacks of cups.

"Sorry, we just wanted actual shot glasses."

"Clearly," I say and clean up the mess.

I'd make him do it, but his stumble on the way out to the patio says he'd probably make the problem worse.

I glance at the clock. It's only nine, and people are already this drunk.

Hell.

I grab the four bottles of hard liquor sitting out and jog them up the stairs to my room. I don't mind sharing, but beer will be just fine for everyone here on out until the night is over. Maybe it'll slow some of these people down.

As I descend the stairs, I glance at the door. The girl in the pink shirt isn't anywhere in sight. But I do spot Hero chatting it up with the girl in the blue dress.

Simon and Beck are playing video games on the couch, and

Graham is trying to read a book while the redhead next to him is basically trying to climb into his lap. I make my way through the kitchen, grab a fresh beer, and head out to the patio where Zane is chugging a red cup at one end of the beer pong table.

It almost feels like we're at a frat party. If it were fall and the semester had started, I'm sure we would be. But tonight is basically just a bunch of college kids who either live here full time or stayed to take classes over the summer.

I chuckle to myself.

Does this mean my house is full of like-minded people who know what they want in life and are eager to get there, or is it full of nerds who like summer school?

"Is something funny?"

With a smirk still on my lips, I turn my gaze to the woman who spoke next to me, only to come face-to-face with pink shirt girl.

My smile widens.

"Hi," I say instead of answering her question.

Under the patio lights, I can faintly spot the light pink color in her cheeks.

"Hi," she replies.

Before I can say anything else, a Ping-Pong ball smacks her in the temple. For obvious reasons, she's not injured, but it does startle her enough that she drops her drink.

Her beer spills onto the ground between us.

"Sorry!" Zane yells. "But I get a free pass tonight!"

I grab the ball and toss it back hard enough that it pegs him in the forehead.

Pink shirt girl laughs.

"Sorry, my friends are kind of crazy," I say. "That one just

got his first book deal, and he's going insane right now to celebrate."

She smiles wide. "You hang out with people who write books?"

"Don't sound so surprised."

"It's just weird is all. I mean, college guys barely read, and here you are with someone who writes actual books."

Her tone is flirty, and the smile she gives me hits me right in the heart.

I fucking like that smile.

"Oh, stereotyping, are we?" I flirt back, crossing my arms and widening my stance as I wait for her reply.

She shakes her head.

"Nope. Just speaking from experience to all the college guys I've met so far."

I chuckle, wink at her, and then lean closer. "Want me to blow your mind?"

She laughs, and my heart swells.

I've never heard a laugh that physically gives me energy. I want to hear it again.

"Is that a sex joke I don't get?"

"No." I step even closer to her.

I swear she leans in too.

"Actually," I say in a whisper, "I write too."

"No, you don't. You're just trying to impress me after the comment I just made."

"It's the truth. Me and my friends. There are six of us. We all write romance."

Her smile twitches like she isn't sure if she should smile or laugh or just walk away because I'm now that weird guy.

"Prove it," she says, and honestly, that wasn't what I was expecting her to say. "Let me read something you wrote."

"Seriously?"

"Yeah"—she bumps my shoulder— "or I'll think it's just a line you give to get into a girl's pants."

"All right." I hold out my hand. "Follow me."

"Where to?"

"My room."

"Oh no, I set myself up for that one, didn't I?" But she follows me.

"I'll be a true gentleman," I tell her. "Unless you tell me to be different."

"What a gentlemanly thing to say."

I tug her behind me through the kitchen and up the stairs. Just as we reach my door, I turn to face her.

"By the way, I'm Tobias. What's your name?"

She blushes as I open the door.

"Natalie."

They're best friends, and she's engaged to someone else. Will Tobias figure it out before it's too late?

Find out in Always Been Write.

BONUS EPILOGUE

SIMON

Greer screams louder than I'd ever heard her scream before.

Hell, I'm screaming, too, but it never gets old watching her.

The entire crowd is in an uproar as Grey's football team wins their first game of the season.

My son, our son, has officially won his first college game as the quarterback.

This is a moment I'll never forget.

"Let's go," I say to Greer as students start to run onto the field.

"No, we have to see him," she says with the proudest smile.

The student section begins to race onto the field in celebration, and as much as I want to see him, too, Grey's going to be busy for the rest of the night.

"We told him we would see him for breakfast in the morning," I remind her.

"Yeah, but this is so exciting." She turns to face me, her

eyes glossy. "That little boy who asked me to play football in his backyard all those years ago is in college, Simon. College!"

"I know, baby." I pull her to me so that I can kiss her forehead.

"He won't need me anymore," she adds.

"Oh, he's going to need you plenty," I tell her, lacing our hands together and pulling her through the crowd.

She groans, and I barely hear it over the noise of the stadium. "How is he in college?"

I chuckle. She's repeated this at least a dozen times on the way here. I would have loved for Grey to stay in Wind Valley to go to school. Hell, he might be a young man now, but he's still that ten-year-old kid who would race up and down the stairs, playing video games and football in the backyard. The same kid who, when Greer and I sat him down and told him we were getting married just after his twelfth birthday, said, "You're welcome."

I smile, thinking back to that day. To our life since we said I do. To the day after our wedding when Greer told me she was pregnant and the day we found out it was twin girls. To a thirteen- year-old boy holding his sisters for the first time. All the way to the fact that Greer thinks we're here just for the game.

Greer chatters about how proud she is of Grey the entire way to the car and the entire way to the hotel.

I pull up and the valet comes out, opening her door. She gets out and then pauses when I come around the front of our rental car.

"Simon, what are we doing here?" she says in a whisper. "This place is really, really fancy."

I slide my hand across her lower back, pulling her to me. She rests a hand on my chest.

"We're staying here for the weekend."

"What?"

"Yep, you heard me. All weekend. Tomorrow, after breakfast, we have a couple's massage, followed by an entire day of pampering and then one more night of just the two of us."

She bites her bottom lip.

"But we need to get back to the girls. We told your sister we'd be gone only one night."

Yep, our five-year-olds are probably destroying my sister's house. I also know she's likely loving every minute of it.

"Calla and Beck have them."

Her eyes light up as she lifts onto her toes to press her lips to mine. She lets out a moan and perks up. "Do we get to sleep in in the morning? And you said massages?"

I nod, answering both of her questions.

"Well, what are we waiting for?" She grabs my hands and pulls me into the lobby, straight for the reception desk.

Greer is scrolling the hotel's spa listing as we step into the elevator.

"Oh, they have a restaurant on the floor below the spa. I didn't bring anything fancy, but do you want to grab a drink or snack once we freshen up?"

She looks up, waiting for my answer, but the look on my face must say enough.

"Mmm," she says and clicks her phone off, dropping it into her purse before wrapping her arms around my waist. "I'm pretty sure that's the look you gave me the night we made the girls."

I chuckle.

I don't plan on making more kids tonight, but I sure as hell plan to recreate everything about that night and any other night I have Greer in my arms.

The doors open, and with my wife under my arms, I lead us to our room for the night, where I plan for a very, *very* late night.

If you'd have asked me seven years ago where I pictured my life, I'd never have said spending a weekend away with Greer after watching our son play football in college while my sister watches our twins back in Wind Valley. That would have been the furthest thing from my mind, but hell, these days, I'm rooting for everyone to take chances.

Falling in love with Greer was the best thing that has ever happened to me.

They're best friends, and she's engaged to someone else. Will Tobias figure it out before it's too late?

Find out in the next and final Wind Valley book, Always Been Write.

MORE BOOKS BY JAMI ROGERS

For the full list of titles by Jami Rogers, please scan the QR code below.

ABOUT THE AUTHOR

My name is Jami Rogers, and I write small-town, steamy romance. My favorite tropes to write (and read) are enemies to lovers, friends to lovers, roommates, and my best friend's brother/sister.

I like to read, write, watch movies/TV, and spend time with my family. I'm horrible at returning phone calls and prefer to text, but still struggle to hit the little blue arrow to send a message once I'm finished typing my reply. My husband does 90% of the cooking in our house. Not because I'm busy – I'm just simply a bad cook.

facebook.com/AuthorJamiRogers

instagram.com/authorjamirogers

goodreads.com/jamirogers

bookbub.com/profile/jami-rogers

tiktok.com/@authorjamirogers

* 9 7 9 8 9 9 0 0 9 5 4 0 3 *